# Also by Stuart Gibbs

**The FunJungle series**
*Belly Up*
*Poached*
*Big Game*
*Panda-monium*
*Lion Down*
*Tyrannosaurus Wrecks*
*Bear Bottom*
*Whale Done*

**The Spy School series**
*Spy School*
*Spy Camp*
*Evil Spy School*
*Spy Ski School*
*Spy School Secret Service*
*Spy School Goes South*
*Spy School British Invasion*
*Spy School Revolution*
*Spy School at Sea*
*Spy School Project X*
*Spy School Goes North*

**with Anjan Sarkar**
*Spy School the Graphic Novel*
*Spy Camp the Graphic Novel*

**The Moon Base Alpha series**
*Space Case*
*Spaced Out*
*Waste of Space*

**The Charlie Thorne series**
*Charlie Thorne and the Last Equation*
*Charlie Thorne and the Lost City*
*Charlie Thorne and the Curse of Cleopatra*
*Charlie Thorne and the Royal Society*

**The Once Upon a Tim series**
*Once Upon a Tim*
*The Labyrinth of Doom*
*The Sea of Terror*
*The Quest of Danger*

*The Last Musketeer*

# STUART GIBBS

ILLUSTRATED BY ANJAN SARKAR

# EVIL spy school

## THE GRAPHIC NOVEL

A spy school NOVEL

Simon & Schuster Books for Young Readers
New York London Toronto Sydney New Delhi

SIMON & SCHUSTER BOOKS FOR YOUNG READERS
An imprint of Simon & Schuster Children's Publishing Division
1230 Avenue of the Americas, New York, New York 10020
This book is a work of fiction. Any references to historical events, real people, or real places are used fictitiously. Other names, characters, places, and events are products of the author's imagination, and any resemblance to actual events or places or persons, living or dead, is entirely coincidental.

Adapted from *Evil Spy School* (2015) by Stuart Gibbs

Interior design by Lucy Ruth Cummins
The text for this book was set in CCSamaritan.
The illustrations for this book were rendered digitally.
Manufactured in China
1123 SCP
10 9 8 7 6 5 4 3 2 1
Library of Congress Cataloging-in-Publication Data
Names: Gibbs, Stuart, 1969– author. | Sarkar, Anjan, illustrator.
Title: Evil spy school the graphic novel / Stuart Gibbs ; illustrated by Anjan Sarkar.
Description: First Simon & Schuster Books for Young Readers hardcover edition. | New York : Simon & Schuster Books for Young Readers, 2024. | Series: Spy school ; book 3 | Audience: Ages 8–12 | Audience: Grades 4–6 |
Summary: After being expelled from spy school, thirteen-year-old Ben Ripley accepts an offer to join evil crime organization SPYDER, and although he knows he is a key part of their sinister plan he is not sure how to get word to the good guys without being caught.
Identifiers: LCCN 2022038485 (print) | LCCN 2022038486 (ebook) |
ISBN 9781665931946 (hardcover) | ISBN 9781665931939 (paperback) | ISBN 9781665931953 (ebook)
Subjects: CYAC: Graphic novels. | Spies—Fiction. | Schools—Fiction. | LCGFT: Spy comics. | Graphic novels.
Classification: LCC PZ7.7.G5324 Ev 2024 (print) | LCC PZ7.7.G5324 (ebook) |
DDC 741.5/973—dc23/eng/20230131
LC record available at https://lccn.loc.gov/2022038485
LC ebook record available at https://lccn.loc.gov/2022038486

In memory of Emily Normandin-Parker —S. G.

For Yukihiro and Tokuro —A. S.

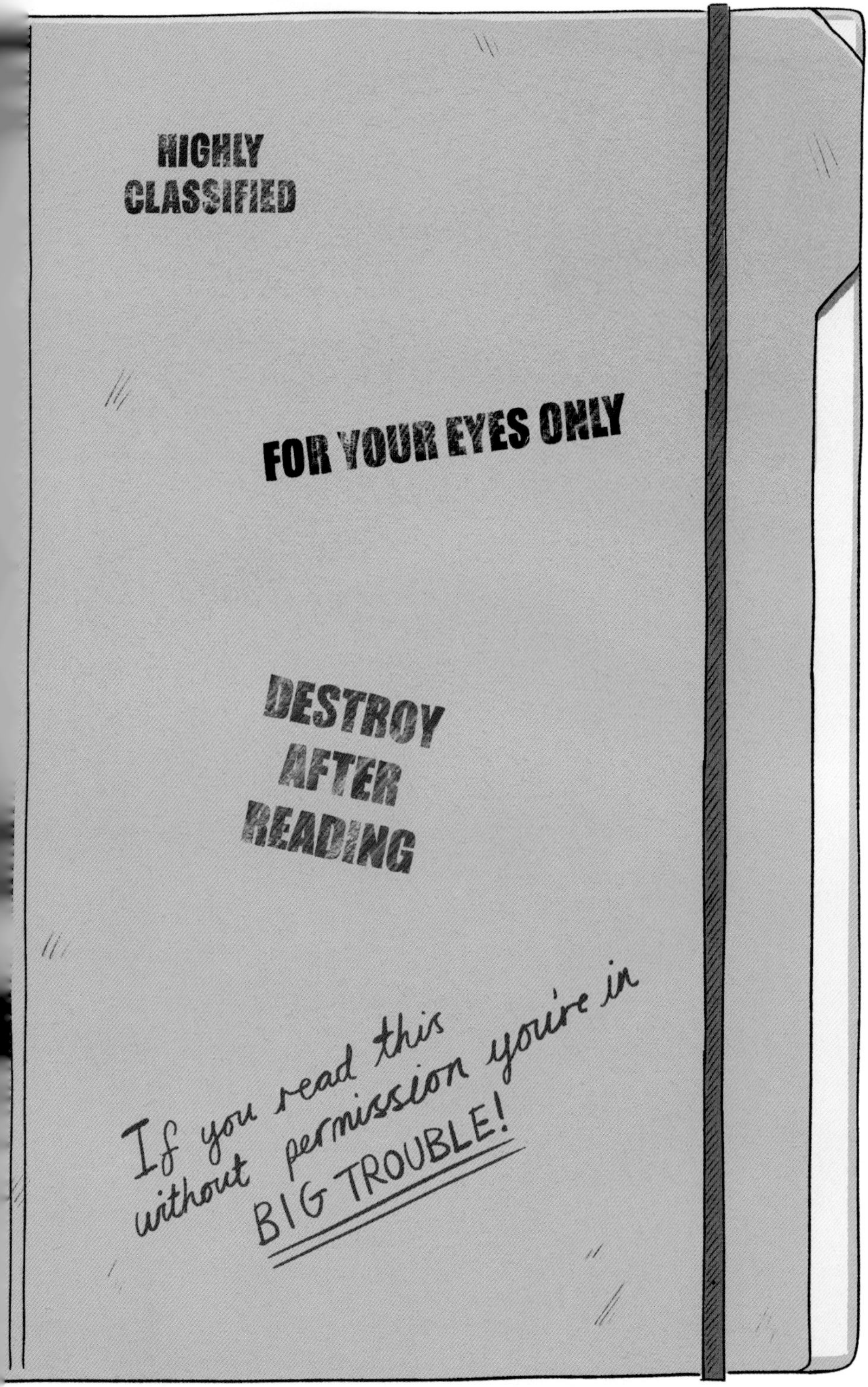

HIGHLY
CLASSIFIED

FOR YOUR EYES ONLY

DESTROY
AFTER
READING

If you read this
without permission you're in
BIG TROUBLE!

**Name:** Benjamin Ripley

**Age:** 13

**Year at the academy:** Second

**Code name:** Smokescreen

**Mental acuity:** Very intelligent. Level 16 math skills.

**Physical ability:** Not so much.

Recruited to the Academy of Espionage last January as part of Operation Creeping Badger. Ripley was only supposed to be bait to lure out the mole on campus—but he surprised us all by actually being competent enough to find the mole, defeat SPYDER, and survive (although he had some help).

Then, last summer, SPYDER attempted another evil scheme, which Ripley was also instrumental in thwarting.

He might actually have some potential as a field agent.

**Name:** Murray Hill

**Age:** 13

**Year at the academy:** No longer valid

**Code name:** Washout

**Mental acuity:** Not bad; very sneaky and underhanded

**Physical ability:** Embarrassing

Murray Hill flunked his first year at the academy and then spent much of his second year working as a covert mole for SPYDER. Thanks to Operation Creeping Badger, he was apprehended, but SPYDER moles at the CIA freed him before he could be incarcerated. He was then a key player in SPYDER's next evil plot—although, thanks to the work of Agents-in-Training Hale and Ripley, he was apprehended again. And this time, he is actually incarcerated. Really.

**Name:** Erica Hale

**Age:** 15

**Year at the academy:** Fourth

**Code name:** Ice Queen

**Mental acuity:** Excellent

**Physical ability:** Off the charts

Despite only being a fourth-year student, Hale is easily the best student at the academy. This can be attributed, in part, to the fact that she is a legacy: The Hale family can be traced back to Nathan and Elias Hale, spies for the Colonial forces during the American Revolution. Thus, the Hales have been spying for the United States since before there was a United States.

Erica is adept in five forms of martial arts, can speak six languages, and has familiarity with a great variety of weapons. However, her interpersonal skills are somewhat lacking. She is regarded by her fellow students (and much of the faculty) as cold, impersonal, and kind of scary.

She was integral to the success of both recent missions where SPYDER was thwarted.

**Name:** Agent Alexander Hale

**Age:** Classified

**Code names:** Gray Wolf, Alpha Dog, Blazing Stallion, Vengeful Lion

**Mental acuity:** Not as good as we originally thought

**Physical ability:** Even worse than the mental acuity

Alexander Hale is the father of Erica Hale and the son of Cyrus Hale. Sadly, he appears to be proof that talent sometimes skips a generation.

Until recently, everyone at the CIA thought this might not be the case. Agent Hale had a long list of successful missions that, it turned out, he hadn't contributed much to. He had either taken the credit for someone else's work—or made much of the mission up. However, we are onto his wily ways now—and he has fallen from grace at the Agency.

**Name:** Cyrus Hale

**Age:** Classified (but pretty old)

**Code name:** Klondike

**Mental acuity:** Excellent (though he's rather crotchety)

**Physical ability:** Excellent (especially for an old guy)

Cyrus was one of the finest agents ever to serve at the CIA up until his retirement. He was forced to reactivate during SPYDER's last mission and has refused to deactivate again.

MISSING IN ACTION

**Name:** Joshua Hallal

**Age:** 17

**Nickname:** Mastermind

**Mental acuity:** Dangerously devious

**Physical ability:** Used to be excellent; may now be compromised.

Hallal was one of the finest agents-in-training at the academy until he was apparently killed by enemy agents in his fifth year. He was presumed dead—until he resurfaced recently as a high-ranking member of SPYDER. Turns out, he was working for the bad guys all along and only faked his own death.

While attempting to escape the agency when his last evil plot was thwarted, he appeared to die in a bizarre mining accident. But we're not buying it this time.

ZOE ZIBBELL "Double Z"
second year

WARREN REEVES "Chameleon"
second year

CHIP SCHACTER "Meathead"
fifth year

JAWAHARLAL O'SHEA "Jawa"
third year

August 30

To: From:
Re: Smokescreen

My covert field research has confirmed the worst. SPYDER definitely has a new diabolical plot underway—and they have started to staff it. Steps must be taken immediately to determine and

Given that the three of us are known to SPYDER and thus unable to infiltrate their organization effectively—and that the CIA has certainly been compromised by enemy agents—we are left with no choice but to activate Benjamin Ripley for Operation Bedbug.

This mission is unsanctioned and unapproved. It is not to be discussed with anyone, anywhere, no matter how much you think you can trust them. This is especially true for For his own safety, even young Mr. Ripley cannot be informed of what is truly going on until we are sure that

If anyone has any doubts about Mr. Ripley's ability to serve in this capacity, now is the time to voice them. The consequences of his failure on this mission would be disastrous.

Unless I hear from you, the mission will commence on September 3 at 1100 hours.

God bless America,

BOOM!

AAAAAAAAAAAAAA

AAAAAAAAAAAH!!
ONCE WE CATCH YOU, YOU'RE DONE FOR, RIPLEY!
WHIZZ!
WHIZZ!
ERICA! I'M COMING IN HOT!
OKAY. I'M READY.
ULTIMATE SOLDIER
WHIZZ!

WOOSH!
AAAARRGH!
SKID!
SPLAT!

BOOM!
SPLAT!
YOU WALKED RIGHT INTO THE AMBUSH, ALICE. AN F FOR SELF-PRESERVATION.
RED TEAM, YOU CALL THAT A COORDINATED ATTACK? THAT'S B-MINUS WORK FOR SURE!

BOOM!
BANG!
WHAT'S HAPPENING IN THERE? IT SOUNDS DANGEROUS.
THE STUDENTS ARE, UH...
...STUDYING COMBUSTION IN CHEMISTRY TODAY. DON'T WORRY. IT'S COMPLETELY SAFE.
ST. SMITHEN'
SCIENCE ACADE
ESTABLISHED
1802

SOME OF THEM ARE *AWFULLY BIG* TWELVE-YEAR-OLDS.
HOW MANY OF THEM ARE THERE?

SEVEN.
RAAAAAAAA AAAAAA!!

CRUNCH!
SPLAT!

SPLAT!
SPLAT!
SPLAT!
SPLOP!

NOW THERE'S ONLY TWO.
DID YOU ONLY HAVE FIVE PAINTBALLS?

NO. I HAVE PLENTY.

THEN WHY DIDN'T YOU TAKE OUT ALL SEVEN ENEMY AGENTS?

WHAT FUN WOULD THAT BE?

RAA! RAA!

DUFF!

SLAM!

SPLAT!

BLAM!

SHOVE!
ARGHH!

STOP! I QUIT!
YOU QUIT? ER...I DON'T THINK YOU CAN DO THAT.
I THOUGHT I COULD HACK IT HERE, BUT I WAS WRONG. THIS IS TOO HARD!
I WANT TO GO HOME! I WANT MY MOMMY!

SORRY. SPY SCHOOL'S NOT FOR EVERYONE...

LIKE YOU?

WHACK!

CATCH!

SAY YOUR PRAYERS, RIPLEY!
NICE TRY, NEWBIE. BUT YOU'RE OUT.
BLAM! BLAM!
SPLAT!
YOU GOT LUCKY THIS TIME. NEXT TIME, YOUR GIRLFRIEND MIGHT NOT BE AROUND TO SAVE YOU.

I'M NOT HIS GIRLFRIEND!
BOOM!
MAN, THAT KID WAS DEVIOUS.
SHE WAS. SHE'LL DO WELL HERE.
YOU KNOW, WHEN NORMAL KIDS GO BACK TO SCHOOL, THEIR FIRST DAY IS ALL ABOUT GETTING ORIENTED AND MEETING THEIR TEACHERS. THERE'S NO PAINT GUNS OR PRETEND WARS.
REALLY? IT MUST SUCK TO BE NORMAL.

CHAMELEON DOESN'T KNOW HOW TO WORK THE MORTAR.

YES I DO!

TAKE COVER!

BOOM!

SPLAT!

SPLAT!

YOU GUYS NEARLY TOOK US OUT JUST NOW!
SORRY. MY BAD.

ALL RIGHT. I'M BRINGING SMOKESCREEN IN.

STAY BEHIND ME.

BLAM!
BLAM!
CRACK!
SPLAT!
SMACK!
DOFF!
BLAM!
SPLAT!

THANK GOODNESS YOU'RE HERE.

WHAT'S THE PROBLEM?

WE'RE TRYING TO TAKE OUT THE ENEMY MORTAR BASE, BUT WE CAN'T GET THE TARGETING RIGHT.

WE'LL HANDLE IT.
MOVE. YOU'RE IN MY SPACE.

DO YOU NEED THIS?
FIRING MORTARS (FOR DUMMIES)

PLEASE. I'VE KNOWN HOW TO OPERATE A MORTAR SINCE I WAS IN PRESCHOOL.

HOW FAR IS THE ENEMY BASE?

ONE HUNDRED SIXTY-FIVE METERS.

WEIGHT OF THE SHELL?

IS THAT IMPORTANT?
ONLY IF YOU ACTUALLY WANT TO TAKE OUT THE ENEMY RATHER THAN OUR OWN TEAM.

STANDARD SHELL WEIGHS SIXTEEN POUNDS.

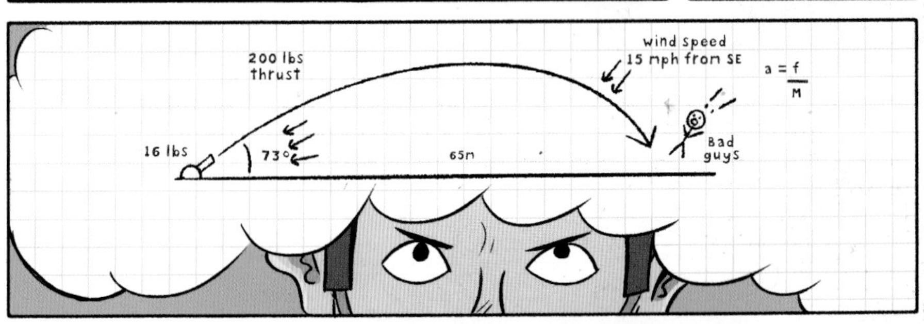
200 lbs thrust
wind speed 15 mph from SE
a = f / M
16 lbs
73°
65m
Bad guys

WE NEED A LAUNCH ANGLE OF SEVENTY-THREE DEGREES, AIMING SIX DEGREES TO THE RIGHT OF THE TARGET.
ROGER.

PAINT SHELL SAFE FOR COMBAT SIMULATIONS
PAINT SHELL SAFE FOR COMBAT SIMULATIONS
PAINT SHELL SAFE FOR COMBAT SIMULATIONS

I'LL HANDLE THAT! FIRING THIS IS *MY* JOB!

ARE YOU SURE YOU'RE RIGHT, BEN? IF WE DON'T TAKE OUT THEIR MORTAR WITH THIS SHOT, THEY'LL WIN WITH THEIR NEXT BLAST.
BLAM!

HEY, WHEN IT COMES TO MATH, SMOKESCREEN IS NEVER WRONG.

IT'LL WORK.

READY TO LAUNCH!

WAIT!
WHAT'S WRONG?

THAT KNUCKLEHEAD PUT A LIVE ROUND IN THERE!

HELP! SHE'S A DOUBLE AGENT FOR THE RED TEAM!

DUFF!
FIRE!
CLICK!

BOOM!
WOOSH!
UH-OH.

BOOM!

WHAT'S THE CHANCE THAT THE PRINCIPAL WAS UP THERE?
WELL, HE'S *SUPPOSED* TO BE DOWN HERE IN THE REVIEWING STANDS. BUT THE CHANCES OF THE PRINCIPAL BEING IN THE RIGHT PLACE AT THE RIGHT TIME AREN'T USUALLY VERY GOOD.

AAARRRRRGGGHHH!!

WHO IS RESPONSIBLE FOR THIS? FIND THEM AND BRING THEM TO ME!
OOOH, BEN, YOU'RE IN TROUBLE!

FIVE MINUTES LATER...

LOOK AT THIS ROOM! LOOK WHAT YOU DID TO IT! DO YOU SEE WHAT YOU'VE DONE TO MY DESK?

ER...NO. YOUR DESK ISN'T THERE ANYMORE.

EXACTLY! THAT DESK WAS A PRICELESS ARTIFACT—AND YOU DESTROYED IT!
I'M SORRY. I WASN'T *TRYING* TO HIT YOUR OFFICE.

I WAS TRYING TO PREVENT SOME STUDENTS FROM GETTING BLOWN UP.
WHY WERE YOU EVEN FIRING LIVE AMMUNITION DURING A FAKE BATTLE IN THE FIRST PLACE?

AND YOU AIMED IT AT A BUILDING INSTEAD? BECAUSE THE WHOLE POINT OF BUILDINGS IS THAT THEY GENERALLY HAVE PEOPLE INSIDE THEM.

NOT TODAY. THIS BUILDING WAS SUPPOSED TO BE EMPTY. THE SACSA EXAMS WERE MANDATORY FOR ALL STUDENTS AND FACULTY.

WHAT NINCOMPOOP SAID THAT?

UH...*YOU* DID.

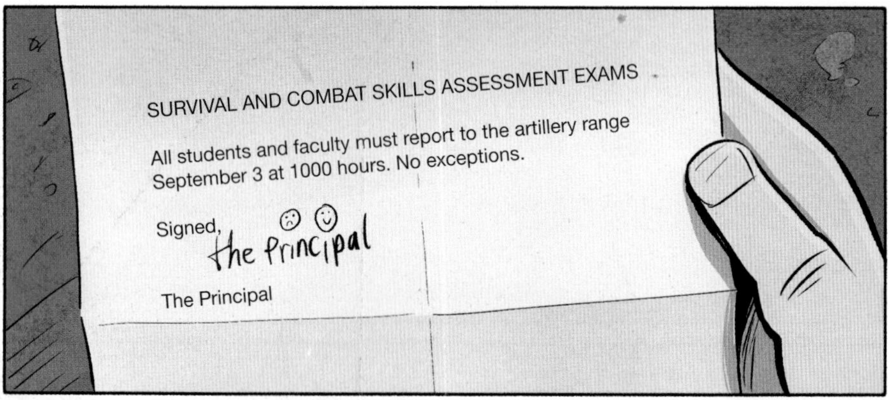
SURVIVAL AND COMBAT SKILLS ASSESSMENT EXAMS

All students and faculty must report to the artillery range September 3 at 1000 hours. No exceptions.

Signed,
the Principal

The Principal

YOU'RE EXPELLED FROM SCHOOL!
RIP!
WHAT?! WHY?
BECAUSE YOU BLEW UP MY OFFICE! YOU HONESTLY THINK I'D LET YOU STAY HERE AFTER A SCREWUP LIKE THIS?
YOUR BEHAVIOR WAS RASH AND POORLY THOUGHT OUT–

THERE WAS NO TIME TO THINK!

THAT'S NEVER STOPPED ME. I RARELY TAKE TIME TO THINK AT ALL, AND YET YOU DON'T SEE ME BLOWING UP PEOPLE'S OFFICES.

SO, IF I HAD JUST STOOD THERE AND LET THOSE OTHER STUDENTS GET HURT, THEN I WOULDN'T BE GETTING EXPELLED RIGHT NOW?

LOOK, I'M NOT IN FAVOR OF HURTING STUDENTS. IN FACT, I'M AGAINST IT. BUT WE ARE TRAINING PEOPLE TO BE SPIES HERE, AND THE CIA NEEDS PEOPLE WHO WON'T CRACK UNDER PRESSURE...
PEOPLE WHO CAN SAVE LIVES WITHOUT HARMING OTHER PEOPLE WHILE THEY ARE INNOCENTLY USING THE BATHROOM–
I MEAN, DOING IMPORTANT WORK IN THEIR OFFICES!

I *HAVE* HELD UP UNDER PRESSURE. IN FACT, I'VE DONE IT *TWICE*. I DEFEATED THE PLANS OF SPYDER TWO TIMES...
SPYDER?
THE EXTREMELY SECRETIVE EVIL ORGANIZATION THAT CAUSES CHAOS AND MAYHEM ON A GRAND SCALE FOR A PRICE?

THEY TRIED TO BLOW UP THIS SCHOOL TWO MONTHS AGO–ALONG WITH THE HEADS OF EVERY ESPIONAGE AGENCY IN THE USA...
0:00

ONLY I THWARTED THEM, SAVING DOZENS OF LIVES—INCLUDING YOURS.
THWUMP!
AND THEN, LAST SUMMER, I THWARTED THEIR PLANS TO DESTROY THE LEADERS OF A DOZEN COUNTRIES, INCLUDING THE PRESIDENT OF THE UNITED STATES.
KRING!
THERE ARE ACTUAL AGENTS WHO HAVEN'T DONE WHAT I HAVE. AND AFTER ALL THAT, YOU'RE EXPELLING ME?!
YOU MIGHT HAVE DEFEATED SPYDER, BUT YOU ARE ALSO RECKLESS, DANGEROUS, AND INSUBORDINATE.
THERE IS NO PLACE AT THIS SCHOOL FOR STUDENTS LIKE YOU!

James Kagan
Dean of
Survival Skills

HELLO, BENJAMIN. HOW'S YOUR FIRST DAY OF THE SCHOOL YEAR GOING?

NOT SO GOOD. I JUST GOT EXPELLED.
FOR WHAT?
I SORT OF BLEW UP THE PRINCIPAL'S OFFICE.

OH. SO THAT'S WHAT THAT LOUD BOOM WAS. WELL, WE ALL FALL FROM GRACE SOONER OR LATER, DON'T WE?
I WOULD HAVE PREFERRED LATER.

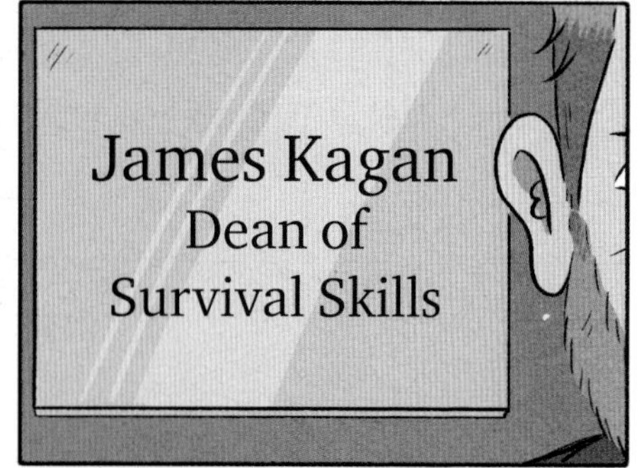
James Kagan
Dean of
Survival Skills

IS ALL THAT STUFF YOURS?

ER...KIND OF. KAGAN FILCHED PLENTY FROM ME OVER THE YEARS. I CAN'T EVEN COUNT HOW MANY BULLETS I LENT HIM.
BUT WAS HE THERE WHEN I NEEDED SOMEONE TO STAND UP FOR ME? NO.

SO AT THE VERY LEAST, HE OWES ME A STAPLER.

I REALLY SHOULD GO. IF ANYONE ASKS, YOU NEVER SAW ME.

I CAN'T BELIEVE THEY'RE BOOTING YOU FOR THIS.
HOW'D YOU EVEN KNOW? THE PRINCIPAL JUST TOLD ME...
WE'RE STUDYING TO BE SPIES. IT'S OUR JOB TO KNOW THINGS.

YOU WANT TO GET EVEN WITH THE PRINCIPAL? I'D BE HAPPY TO DO THAT FOR YOU. JUST SAY THE WORD AND HIS CAR ENDS UP IN THE POTOMAC RIVER.
THANKS FOR THE OFFER. BUT I'LL PASS.

WE SHOULD WRITE A PETITION OR SOMETHING! AND WE COULD SEND IT TO THE TOP BRASS AT THE CIA TOO!

THEY SHOULD KNOW THEY'RE LOSING ONE OF THEIR BEST SPIES-TO-BE FOR A RIDICULOUS REASON.
IF ANYONE SHOULD HAVE BEEN BOOTED FOR DESTROYING THE PRINCIPAL'S OFFICE, IT'S WARREN.
NOD NOD!
NOD NOD!
HEY! THIS ISN'T MY FAULT!

YOU LOADED THE MORTAR.

THERE WERE ONLY SUPPOSED TO BE PAINT BOMBS IN THE AMMO PILE. I'M NOT THE FOOL WHO PUT A LIVE SHELL IN THERE WITH THEM.

BUT YOU *ARE* THE FOOL WHO DIDN'T NOTICE THE DIFFERENCE.

YOU REALLY SCREWED UP.

*ME?* DON'T YOU MEAN THE PRINCIPAL?

NO. YOU CRACKED UNDER PRESSURE AND MADE A HUGE MISTAKE. YES, YOU SAVED SOME PEOPLE, BUT IN DOING SO, YOU NEARLY KILLED SOMEONE ELSE.
WHO KNOWS WHAT MIGHT HAVE HAPPENED IF YOU'D BEHAVED LIKE THIS ON A *REAL* MISSION.

BUT YOU'VE BEEN WITH ME ON A REAL MISSION. AND I DIDN'T SCREW UP THEN!

THAT'S NOT EXACTLY TRUE. IN FACT, YOU MADE PLENTY OF MISTAKES ON THOSE MISSIONS. SORRY, BEN, BUT IT DOESN'T LOOK LIKE YOU HAVE WHAT IT TAKES TO BE A SPY.

TAKE MY ADVICE. THE NEXT TIME SOMEONE COMES TO YOU WITH AN OFFER TO CHANGE YOUR LIFE, ACCEPT IT–
AND THEN TRY NOT TO MESS IT UP LIKE YOU DID THIS TIME.

SPIN!
ALL OF YOU KNOW THE RULES. AFTER TODAY, IN ORDER TO PROTECT THE SECRECY OF THIS INSTITUTION, NONE OF YOU CAN HAVE ANY MORE CONTACT WITH BEN.
AS FAR AS THIS SCHOOL IS CONCERNED, BENJAMIN RIPLEY NO LONGER EXISTS.

LOOK AT THE BRIGHT SIDE. AT LEAST WHEN YOU GO BACK TO YOUR OLD MIDDLE SCHOOL, YOU WON'T BE IN DANGER ALL THE TIME.

YOU'VE OBVIOUSLY NEVER BEEN TO MY OLD MIDDLE SCHOOL.

THE NEXT DAY...
LEE MIDDLE
SCHOOL

IT'S GOOD TO HAVE
YOU BACK, BUDDY.

PROD!

IT'S GOOD
TO SEE YOU
AGAIN.

I KNOW YOU'RE BUMMED THAT YOU CAN'T
GO TO THAT SCIENCE SCHOOL ANYMORE,
BUT TRUST ME, IT'S WAY BETTER HERE.
I ALREADY WENT
TO THIS SCHOOL.
IT STUNK.

I'LL TELL YOU WHY THIS IS
BETTER: WE HAVE GIRLS HERE.

SNIFF
SNIFF!

PUSH!

THERE WERE GIRLS AT ST. SMITHEN'S. YOU SAW ERICA. SHE WAS AMAZING.
TRUE. ERICA WAS SMOKING HOT. BUT YOU'RE NOT SEEING HER ANYMORE. YOU KNOW HOW YOU GET OVER LOSING A HOT GIRLFRIEND? YOU GET ANOTHER HOT GIRLFRIEND.

HEY.

YOU ALL REMEMBER BEN, RIGHT?

KIND OF.

MAYBE.

NO.

I'VE BEEN IN THE SAME GRADE WITH ALL OF YOU SINCE KINDERGARTEN!

SHRUG!

BEN JUST TRANSFERRED BACK HERE FROM PRIVATE SCHOOL.
REALLY? WHAT SCHOOL?

ST. SMI–
YOU WOULDN'T HAVE HEARD OF IT. IT'S TOP SECRET.

WHY IS IT SECRET?
BECAUSE BEN WAS COVERTLY TRAINING TO BE A SPY.

LIAR.

HE'S LYING, RIGHT?
YES, HE'S LYING.

I KNEW IT!
COME ON. YOU CAN'T EXPECT HIM TO ADMIT THE TRUTH, CAN YOU?
I THOUGHT YOU WERE AT SOME DORKY SCIENCE ACADEMY.
IT WAS HIS COVER.
IF YOU WERE IN SPY SCHOOL, WHAT ARE YOU DOING BACK HERE?

THAT'S EXACTLY WHAT I'D EXPECT SOMEONE WHO *WAS* TRAINING TO BE A SPY TO SAY.

SPIN!

WHAT ARE YOU DOING?

WHAT ARE *YOU* DOING?

I'M TRYING TO GET YOU A NEW GIRLFRIEND.

BY LYING TO THEM?

YES!

BECAUSE THE WHOLE "I JUST GOT KICKED OUT OF SCIENCE SCHOOL" THING ISN'T GONNA PLAY AS WELL AS A BRILLIANT LIE ABOUT YOU BEING A SPY-IN-TRAINING...

BUT...

SPIN!
SORRY. BEN'S UPSET AT ME FOR BLOWING HIS COVER. APPARENTLY, NOW THAT YOU KNOW THE TRUTH ABOUT HIM, WE'RE ALL IN MORTAL DANGER.

WOOSH!

CRACK!

I HEARD YOU GOT KICKED OUT
OF YOUR SCIENCE SCHOOL.

N-N-NO. I LOST MY
SCHOLARSHIP.

LEAVE HIM ALONE, DIRK.
WHY DO YOU INSIST ON HANGING OUT WITH THIS LOSER, BREZINSKI?

'CAUSE IT'S BETTER THAN HANGING OUT WITH A JERK LIKE YOU. LET HIM GO.

YOU GONNA MAKE ME?
I MIGHT.

MIKE, YOU DON'T HAVE TO DO THIS.

YES I DO. I'M NOT GOING TO LET THIS BOZO RUIN YOUR FIRST DAY BACK.

WOOSH!

SLAP!

ACADEMY
OF ESPIONAGE
INTRODUCTION TO
SELF-PRESERVATION

SWISH!
THE SNEAKY COBRA DEFENSE
DODGE!
THE WILY WEASEL ARM TWIST
TWIST!
THE SPINELESS WORM FACE SPLAT
SPLAT!
ARE YOU GOING TO BEHAVE NOW?
SQUEEZE!
ARRRGH!
YES.

ALL RIGHT THEN.
RAAAAAAAAA!!
ANGRY MONKEY COUNTERATTACK
SWIPE!
SPIN!
DUFF!
CHOP!

WOOP!
WOO!
WOOP!
THUMP!
YOU EXPECT US TO BELIEVE YOU LEARNED *THAT* IN SCIENCE SCHOOL?
KARATE'S REALLY JUST PHYSICS.
WHAT ARE YOU GONNA DO TO THE OTHER THREE GUYS?

WHAT OTHER THREE GUYS?

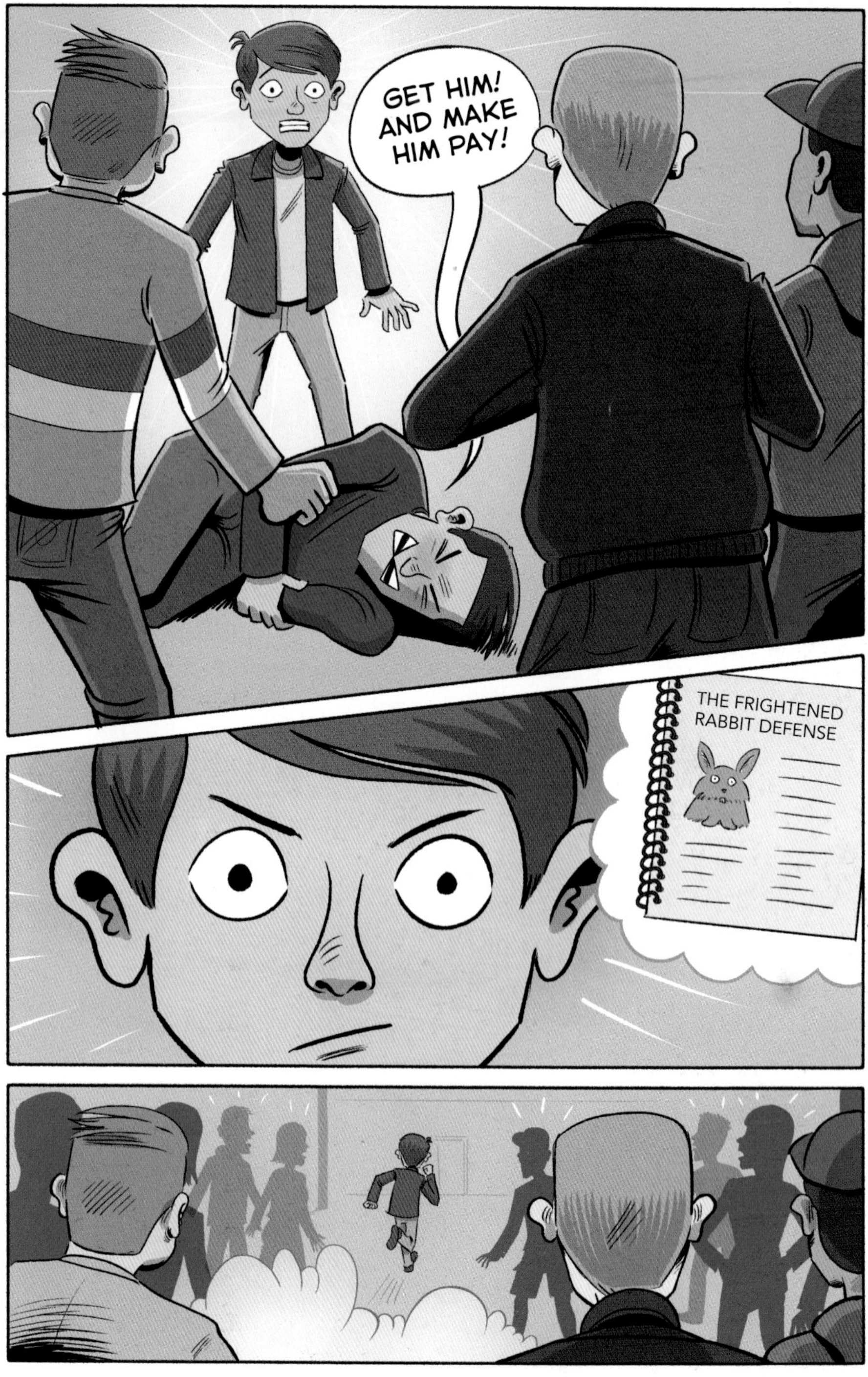

GET HIM!
AND MAKE
HIM PAY!

THE FRIGHTENED
RABBIT DEFENSE

CRASH!
EMERGENCY EXIT ONLY

THMP!
THMP!
THMP!
RATTLE!
RATTLE!
THMP!
THMP!
THMP!
SPIN!
GULP!
SKREECH!
OOFF!!
SMACK!
WHACK!
ARRGH!!
URRGH.

JOSHUA?! I THOUGHT YOU WERE DEAD!

I'M NOT. SURPRISE. I HAVE A PROPOSITION FOR YOU. WE NEED TO TALK.

BUT FIRST, WE NEED TO GET OUT OF HERE.
I THINK THEY WENT THIS WAY! COME ON!

I'M NOT GOING ANYWHERE WITH YOU.

SWISH!
BEEP!

DOES THIS CHANGE YOUR MIND?
YES. IT SURE DOES.

CRASH!

HOLY COW! LOOK AT THIS!

BEN WIPED THE FLOOR WITH THEM!
YOU WEREN'T KIDDING! HE *IS* A SPY!

IS HE DATING ANYONE?

ESPECT

VROOM!

PSST!

THE LAST TIME I SAW YOU, YOU FELL INTO A DEEP RAVINE. HOW'D YOU SURVIVE?
I LANDED IN A BOG. OR A MARSH. SOMETHING SQUISHY. IT BROKE MY FALL ENOUGH TO SAVE MY LIFE.
SPYDER'S AGENTS FOUND ME LATER, AND THE DOCTORS DID THE BEST THEY COULD TO HEAL ME.

IT'S GOOD TO SEE YOU AGAIN, BEN. YOU LOOK LIKE YOU'VE KEPT YOURSELF IN GOOD SHAPE.
THANKS. YOU LOOK... UM...WELL, NOT *GOOD* EXACTLY...

BUT...

I THINK THE WORD YOU'RE LOOKING FOR IS "TERRIBLE."

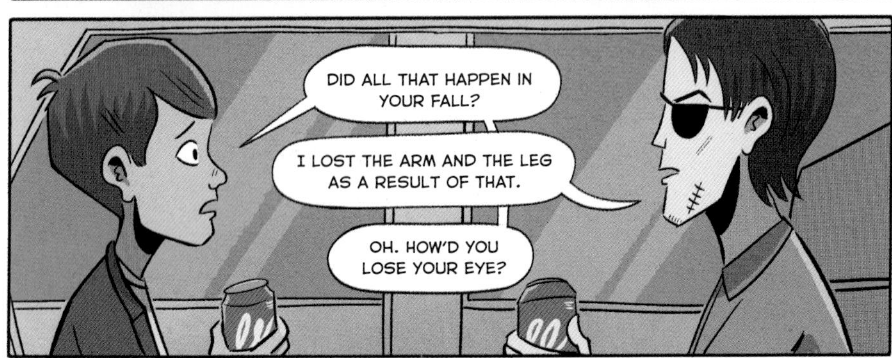
DID ALL THAT HAPPEN IN YOUR FALL?
I LOST THE ARM AND THE LEG AS A RESULT OF THAT.
OH. HOW'D YOU LOSE YOUR EYE?

A BUG FLEW INTO IT.

ER...YOU DON'T LOSE YOUR EYE IF A BUG FLIES INTO IT.

YOU DO IF IT'S YOUR FIRST DAY WITH THE HOOK.

SO, WHAT DO YOU WANT WITH ME?
SPYDER WOULD LIKE YOU TO COME WORK FOR THEM.

YOU GUYS HAVE ALREADY MADE ME THIS OFFER. TWICE. AND I'VE REJECTED YOU TWICE. WHAT MAKES YOU THINK I'M GOING TO ACCEPT THIS TIME?

THE WAY SPY SCHOOL TREATED YOU, FOR STARTERS. YOU'RE ONE OF THE FINEST STUDENTS THEY'VE PRODUCED IN YEARS. AND HOW DO THEY REPAY YOU?

WITH EXPULSION.
WE WOULD TREAT YOU FAR BETTER AT SPYDER. FIRST, WE'D PAY YOU VERY WELL. YOU'LL SOON MAKE MILLIONS WITH US. BUT MORE IMPORTANT, WE'LL GIVE YOU THE RESPECT YOU DESERVE.

WHAT WOULD I BE DOING FOR YOU?

GIVEN YOUR AGE, WE WOULDN'T ACTIVATE YOU RIGHT AWAY. EVEN THOUGH YOU'VE SHOWN SOME METTLE, YOU STILL HAVE THINGS TO LEARN. SO FOR THE TIME BEING, YOU'LL BE SENT TO OUR TRAINING FACILITY.

TRAINING FACILITY?
BEING A BAD GUY ISN'T EASY, YOU KNOW. IN FACT, IT'S CONSIDERABLY HARDER THAN BEING A GOOD GUY. THERE IS A GREAT ARRAY OF SKILLS AND ABILITIES THAT YOU'LL HAVE TO MASTER.
MANY OF THEM ARE SIMILAR TO THOSE YOU BEGAN STUDYING AT THE ACADEMY. OTHERS... LESS SO.

TRAINING MANUAL

TRAINING MANUAL

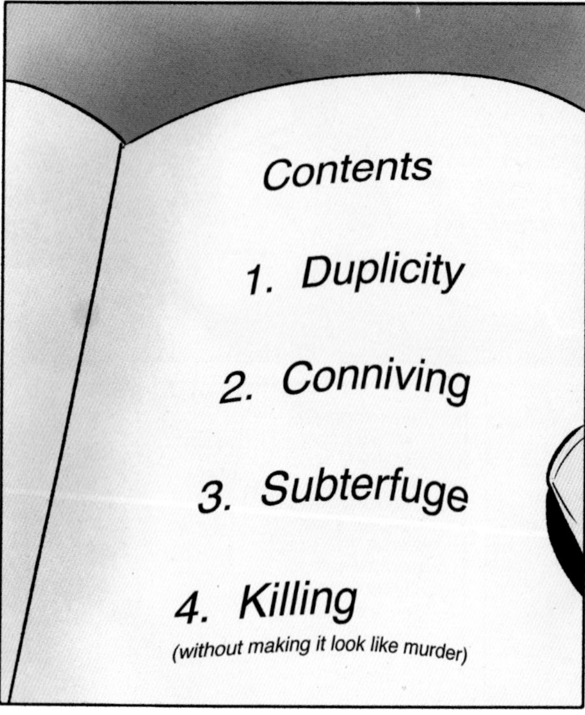
Contents
1. Duplicity
2. Conniving
3. Subterfuge
4. Killing
(without making it look like murder)

SO...IT'S KIND OF LIKE *EVIL SPY SCHOOL*.

I SUPPOSE. ALTHOUGH WE PREFER TO CALL IT THE WISEMAN PREPARATORY ACADEMY.

WHY?
BECAUSE "EVIL SPY SCHOOL" SOUNDS A BIT SUSPICIOUS, DOESN'T IT?

WHERE IS THIS ACADEMY?
YOU DON'T HONESTLY THINK I'D TELL YOU *BEFORE* YOU ACCEPTED OUR OFFER?
SNAP!

I FIGURED IT WAS POSSIBLE...
SHRUG!

I KNOW THIS MIGHT BE A TOUGH DECISION. SO I'LL DO YOU A FAVOR— I'LL GIVE YOU THIRTY SECONDS TO COME TO MAKE UP YOUR MIND.

THE NEXT TIME SOMEONE COMES TO YOU WITH AN OFFER TO CHANGE YOUR LIFE, ACCEPT IT—AND THEN TRY NOT TO MESS IT UP LIKE YOU DID THIS TIME.

TIME'S UP.

I'M IN.
EXCELLENT.
CLINK!

BEEP!
Incapacitate
GAS
PSSSSSS
DONK!

Opportunity is always knocking. Most people just don't open the door.

Opportunity is always knocking. Most people just don't open the door.

WHERE'S MY PHONE...?

ERICA, I HOPE YOU'RE KEEPING AN EYE ON ME. BECAUSE I HAVE NO WAY TO CONTACT YOU FROM HERE.

I WAS ASLEEP FOR SIXTEEN HOURS? WHAT DID THEY GIVE ME?

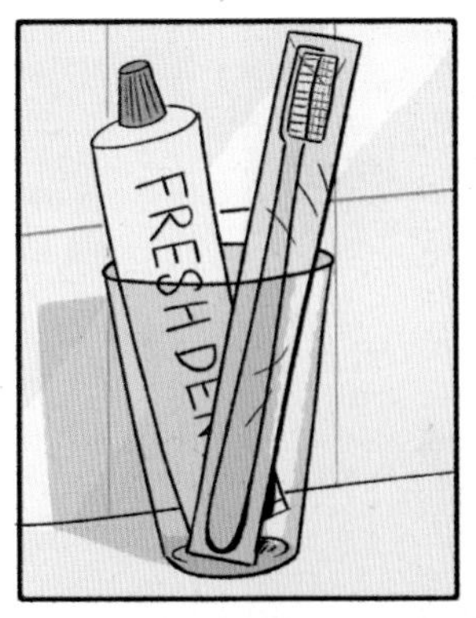
FRESHDEN

A&E
GARDENI
SERVICES

PEW!

PEW!
PEW!
PEW!

PEW!
PEW!
PEW!
KA-
BOOM!

PEW!
PEW!
PEW!
BOOM!

PEW!
SWITCHTOMANUAL CHECKFUELLOWER ALTITUDECIRCLE VICINITY.
PEW!
BOOM!

HI. I'M BEN.
PEW!
ADJUSTALTITUDE EMPLOYBOOSTERSFIND TARGETSREADYMUNITIONS.
PEW!
PEW!
CHEEZ-Os
CRUNCHY

I JUST GOT HERE. I'M NOT SURE WHEN EXACTLY, BECAUSE I WAS DRUGGED. IT'S NICE TO MEET YOU.
EVADEFLAK. LOCKON TARGETSBOMBSAWAY.
PEW!

DO YOU HAVE A NAME?
NEFARIOUS.
PEW!

PEW!
PEW!
PEW!

HIS NAME'S *NEFARIOUS*?

RIGHT. IT'S NOT HIS NICKNAME OR ANYTHING.
IT'S HIS REAL NAME. NEFARIOUS JONES.
PEW!

AND I'M ASHLEY SPARKS. NICE TO MEET YOU.
I'M BEN. BEN RIPLEY.
PEW!
PEW!
PEW!

NO NEED TO INTRODUCE YOURSELF. YOU'RE PRETTY FAMOUS AROUND HERE, GIVEN HOW MUCH TROUBLE YOU'VE CAUSED SPYDER OVER THE LAST YEAR.

OH. SORRY ABOUT THAT.

HEY, YOU DIDN'T THWART *MY* MISSIONS. ANYHOW, IT'S SWAWESOME TO HAVE YOU ON OUR SIDE NOW.

NOT THE CHEEZ-OS!

EXCEPT THE CHEEZ-OS.
NEFARIOUS IS A BIG OLD SCROOGE WITH HIS SNACKS, EVEN THOUGH HE DOESN'T PAY FOR THEM.
SPYDER COVERS OUR BILLS– AND THEY HAVE A STAFF THAT DOES ALL THE SHOPPING FOR US. SO IF YOU WANT ANYTHING, JUST FILL OUT A REQUISITION FORM AND THEY'LL GET IT.

POWER POWDER

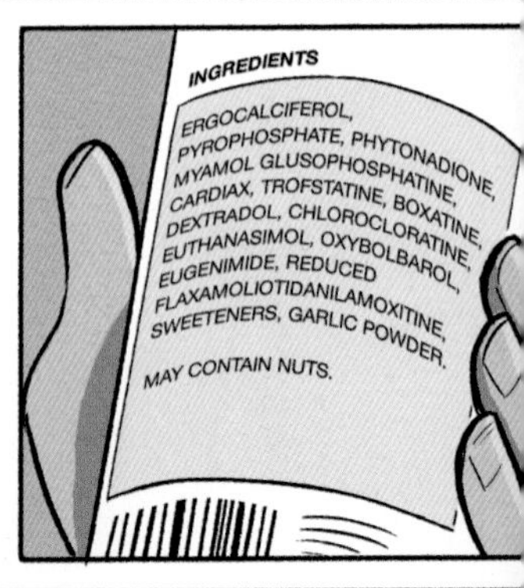
INGREDIENTS
ERGOCALCIFEROL, PYROPHOSPHATE, PHYTONADIONE, MYAMOL GLUSOPHOSPHATINE, CARDIAX, TROFSTATINE, BOXATINE, DEXTRADOL, CHLOROCLORATINE, EUTHANASIMOL, OXYBOLBAROL, EUGENIMIDE, REDUCED FLAXAMOLIOTIDANILAMOXITINE, SWEETENERS, GARLIC POWDER.
MAY CONTAIN NUTS.

WHAT IS THIS STUFF?
POWER POWDER

POWER POWDER! ONE SCOOP PROVIDES ME WITH ALL THE PROBIOTICS, ANTIOXIDANTS, AND DIGESTIVE ENZYMES I NEED EACH DAY–
THOUGH I LIKE TO THROW IN A LITTLE CHIA SEED TO BOOST MY OMEGA-3S. I USE IT TO MAKE ENERGY SHAKES. WANT ONE? THEY'RE TELICIOUS.

TASTY PLUS DELICIOUS?

EXACTLY. AND THEY GIVE YOU A TON OF ENERGY! THEY'RE ALL I EAT, EVERY DAY. YOU'LL LOVE THEM!

SOUNDS GREAT, BUT I'M KIND OF IN THE MOOD FOR CEREAL RIGHT NOW. I ALWAYS WANT CARBS AFTER I'VE BEEN SEDATED.
IS THERE ANY FRUIT?
CORN CRUNCH
UH...NO. AND I THINK WE'RE OUT OF MILK, TOO.
MILK WOULDN'T HAVE DONE YOU ANY GOOD ANYHOW. I JUST REALIZED ALL THE BOWLS ARE DIRTY. THE HOUSEKEEPERS DON'T COME UNTIL TOMORROW.
HOUSEKEEPERS?
YEAH. TO CLEAN UP AFTER US. YOU DIDN'T HAVE MAIDS IN SPY SCHOOL?
ER...NO.
OOH. THAT STINKS.
SO, HAVE YOU HAD A CHANCE TO POKE AROUND YET, OR WOULD YOU LIKE THE TOUR?
A TOUR WOULD BE GREAT. THIS IS AS FAR AS I'VE GOTTEN. I ONLY REGAINED CONSCIOUSNESS A FEW MINUTES AGO.
ARRRGGH!
BOOM!
BAM!
AVOIDENEMYFIRE STAYCALMDEPRESS TRIGGERS.

OBVIOUSLY THIS IS THE LIVING AREA. OUR BEDROOMS ARE ALL UPSTAIRS...
THERE WERE FOUR ROOMS UP THERE. DOES SOMEONE ELSE LIVE HERE?
CORN CRUNCHIES
NOPE. THAT ONE'S EMPTY. IT'S JUST THE THREE OF US. LET'S GO TO THE BASEMENT!
CRUNCH CRUNCH!
CORN

I *WAS.* AND I WAS GOOD, TOO. WATCH!

PLOP!

WHOA. YOU SHOULD HAVE BEEN IN THE OLYMPICS!

YOU'RE RIGHT. I SHOULD HAVE.
I TRIED OUT...BUT ONE LOUSY JUDGE THOUGHT I DIDN'T STICK THE LANDING ON MY DISMOUNT FROM MY UNEVEN BARS ROUTINE... WHEN I DID!
BECAUSE OF HER, I WAS .001 POINTS SHORT OF MAKING THE TEAM. IT TOTALLY BLINKS.
SWISH!
SPIN!
BLOWS PLUS STINKS?
EXACTLY...
DO YOU KNOW WHAT IT'S LIKE TO SPEND YOUR WHOLE LIFE WORKING TOWARD A GOAL...
WOOSH!
FLIP!
...SIXTEEN HOURS A DAY, SEVEN DAYS A WEEK, GIVING UP ANY SEMBLANCE OF A NORMAL LIFE...
...PUTTING EVERYTHING YOU HAVE INTO IT...AND THEN NOT GETTING IT?
THMP!

SORT OF. I JUST GOT BOOTED FROM THE CIA.
WELL, IMAGINE YOU'D BEEN TRAINING FOR THAT SINCE YOU WERE FOUR.
AND THEN GOT ROBBED BY ONE INCOMPETENT JUDGE! I STUCK THAT LANDING! LIKE THIS!
WHIZZ!
SWOOSH!
THMP!

WOW!
CLAP CLAP!
BUT BECAUSE OF THAT JUDGE'S MISTAKE, ALL MY DREAMS WERE SHATTERED.

SO YOU TURNED TO CRIME?

SURE DID! I TOOK ALL THE RAGE AND HATRED AND BAD ENERGY AND REFOCUSED IT INTO THIS.
CRUNCH CRUNCH!
JOSHUA CAME TO RECRUIT ME RIGHT AFTER THE TRIALS.

A FEW MINUTES LATER...
ASHLEY JUST TOLD ME HER STORY. WHAT'S YOURS? WHY ARE YOU STUDYING TO BE A CRIMINAL?

MY PARENTS NAMED ME NEFARIOUS. WHAT ELSE WAS I SUPPOSED TO DO?
BAM!
ARRRGGH!

LET'S GO SEE THE REC CENTER!
THERE'S A REC CENTER?
OH YEAH! IT'S SWAWESOME. WANT TO COME, NEFARIOUS?
MNEH.

OKAY. SEE YOU LATER THEN.
RELOADAMMUNITION SETTARGET ADJUSTALTITUDE.
BOOM!

YOU'RE GOING TO LOVE THE REC. THERE'S A SPA AND BOWLING ALLEYS AND A ROCK-CLIMBING WALL AND A POOL WITH TWO WATER SLIDES!

WOW. OUR POOL AT SPY SCHOOL DIDN'T HAVE WATER SLIDES.

REALLY? WHAT DID IT HAVE?

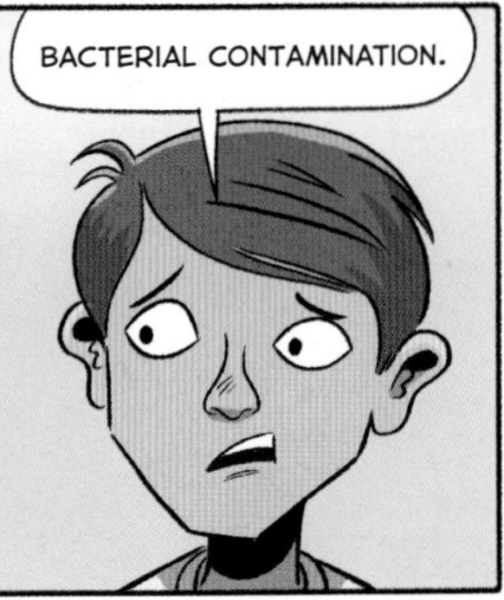
BACTERIAL CONTAMINATION.

WHERE ARE ALL THE OTHER STUDENTS? DO THEY LIVE IN THOSE OTHER HOMES?
THERE ARE NO OTHER STUDENTS.
YOU MEAN... WE'RE THE ENTIRE SCHOOL?
JOSHUA DIDN'T TELL YOU? YEAH, IT'S ONLY US HERE.
HOW LONG HAVE YOU BEEN HERE?
A LITTLE OVER A YEAR. AND NEFARIOUS CAME A FEW MONTHS BEFORE ME.
AND IT'S ONLY BEEN THE TWO OF YOU TRAINING THE WHOLE TIME?
YEAH. SO IT'S PRETTY EXCITING TO HAVE SOMEONE NEW HERE. SOMEONE FUN.
HOW DO YOU KNOW I'M FUN?
ANYONE'S FUN COMPARED TO NEFARIOUS. THE GUY HAS THE PERSONALITY OF AN EGGPLANT.
DOES HE DO ANYTHING BESIDES PLAY VIDEO GAMES?
NOT MUCH. YOU GOT MORE WORDS OUT OF HIM JUST NOW THAN I HAVE IN THE LAST MONTH.

AND HOW DOES DOING GYMNASTICS COUNT AS TRAINING FOR YOU?

BOY, YOU'RE JUST FULL OF QUESTIONS, AREN'T YOU?

I'M NEW HERE. NO ONE'S TOLD ME ANYTHING.

IF WE'RE THE ONLY STUDENTS HERE, WHO ARE ALL THOSE HOMES FOR? OUR TEACHERS?
SOME OF THEM. THOUGH OUR TEACHERS AREN'T *JUST* TEACHERS, LIKE AT YOUR OLD SCHOOL.
THEY ALL HAVE REAL JOBS FOR SPYDER, DOING ALL SORTS OF IMPORTANT STUFF FOR OUR PROJECTS, BUT THEY TAKE A LITTLE TIME EVERY WEEK TO TEACH US ABOUT THEIR AREAS OF EXPERTISE.

SO...THERE'S MORE TO THIS PLACE THAN JUST THE SCHOOL?

OH BOY, YES. A LOT MORE. THIS IS SPYDER'S WORLD HEADQUARTERS.

HIDING IN PLAIN SIGHT.

DOES EVERYONE WHO WORKS FOR SPYDER LIVE HERE?
OF COURSE NOT, SILLYPANTS. SPYDER HAS OPERATIVES ALL OVER THE WORLD.
BUT THIS IS COMMAND CENTRAL, THE HEART OF THE ORGANIZATION. ALL THE IMPORTANT STUFF HAPPENS RIGHT HERE.

ANY IDEA WHERE WE ARE, EXACTLY?
I'M NOT AUTHORIZED TO DIVULGE THAT INFORMATION AT THIS TIME. SORRY.

I'M GUESSING THAT I CAN'T JUST WALK OUT THE FRONT GATE, EITHER.
NOW WHY WOULD YOU WANT TO DO THAT? WE'VE GOT EVERYTHING YOU COULD POSSIBLY WANT RIGHT HERE.

OOH! IT'S TIME FOR CLASS!

I ALMOST FORGOT TO GIVE YOU YOUR SCHEDULE!

TIME TO GET EVIL!

12.00 - 1:15

ADVANCED WEAPONRY WITH COACH SEABROOK

1.15 - 1:30

BREAK (EVIL CONTEMPLATION)

RIPLEY! THERE'S NO WAY IN HECK I'D TRUST YOU WITH A GUN. IN FACT, WITH THOSE HANDS, I'M SURPRISED YOU CAN EVEN USE A FORK.

1:30 - 2:45

BOMB CONSTRUCTION WITH MR. MUKHARJEE

NOW, COMBINE THE TWO VOLATILE CHEMICALS...*VERY CAREFULLY!!* THIS BUILDING WAS JUST BUILT. WE DON'T WANT TO HAVE TO BUILD IT AGAIN!

2.45 - 3:30

PHYSICAL EDUCATION WITH MR. GARABINDIAN

3.30 - 3:45

SNACK

EXCELLENT WORK, ASHLEY!

SMACK!

SNAP!

CRACK!

3:45 - 5:15

EVIL MATHEMATICS WITH MRS. HENDERSON

IF ERNST BLOFELD HAS A THIRTY-TON SURFACE-TO-SURFACE MISSILE AND HE WANTS TO DESTROY A BRIDGE THIRTY-FIVE MILES TO THE NORTH WITH A TWENTY-MILE-PER-HOUR WIND COMING FROM THE EAST...

...HOW MANY POUNDS OF THRUST WILL HE NEED TO LAUNCH THE MISSILE AND DEMOLISH HIS TARGET?

THAT EVENING...

ZZZZZ

LATER...
BEEP! BEEP!
BEEP!
01:15

WAKE UP, BEN. TIME TO FIGURE OUT WHERE THIS PLACE IS.
SLAP!

RATTLE!

ZZZZZZ

PEW!
PEW!
ZZZZZ

CREAK!
PEW!
PEW!
PEW!
WHO'S THERE!?
SPIN!

I'M *TRAPPED* IN THIS HOUSE.
SLAM!

NEXT MORNING...
WHY CAN'T SPYDER GIVE US PHONES? OR INTERNET ACCESS? I CAN'T EVEN DO ANY RESEARCH FOR SCHOOL.
THERE MUST BE A WIRELESS CONNECTION *SOMEWHERE* AROUND HERE, RIGHT?
PAOLO'S
MAYBE. BUT IF THERE IS, I CAN GUARANTEE YOU, WE'RE NOT ALLOWED TO USE IT.
WHY NOT? DOESN'T SPYDER TRUST US?
POWER POWDER
IT'S NOTHING PERSONAL. IT'S FOR OUR PROTECTION. THEY CAN'T JUST LET US ALL SURF THE WEB. BECAUSE ANY LINE OUT IS ALSO A LINE IN.
THE GOVERNMENT COULD USE IT TO ACCESS OUR COMPUTERS AND FIND OUT WHAT WE'RE UP TO.
CLICK!
THERE'S NO WAY THEY CAN GIVE US ANY KIND OF SECURE ACCESS?
I JUST WANT TO SEND MY FOLKS AN EMAIL. LET THEM KNOW THAT I'M OKAY.
OH, YOU'VE BEEN DOING THAT PLENTY.

HOW?

RRRRRRRRRRR

CLICK!

ARE YOU KIDDING? I LOVE THAT I DON'T HAVE TO DEAL WITH MY PARENTS! IT'S ONE OF THE BEST PERKS AT THIS SCHOOL.

I'D BE HAPPY IF I NEVER HAD TO TALK TO MY FOLKS AGAIN.

ADJUSTFLAPSINCOMING MISSILEEVASIVEACTION.

WHAT DO THEY SAY IN THESE EMAILS?
OH, THE STANDARD STUFF, I GUESS. SCHOOL'S GREAT. YOU'RE MAKING FRIENDS. LEARNING A LOT. NOT DOING ANYTHING EVIL AT ALL. BLAH, BLAH, BLAH.
WANT SOME SHAKE?

ER...NO THANKS.

YOU SURE? I MADE PLENTY. AND IT'S SUPER HEALTHY FOR YOU.

MAYBE. BUT IT LOOKS LIKE STUFF THAT OUGHT TO BE COMING *OUT* OF YOU, RATHER THAN GOING IN.

LAUGH NOW, BUT I'M GONNA LIVE TO BE ONE HUNDRED AND FIFTY, DRINKING THIS STUFF.

DOES SPYDER HANDLE ALL COMMUNICATION WITH OUR FRIENDS, TOO?
THEY DO, BUT...IT'S PRETTY HARD TO HAVE FRIENDS ON THE OUTSIDE WHEN YOU WORK FOR SPYDER. SO AFTER A WHILE, SPYDER KIND OF WEEDS THEM ALL OUT OF YOUR LIFE.

WE HAVE TO GIVE UP ALL OUR FRIENDS?

YOU GAVE MOST OF THEM UP WHEN YOU DITCHED SPY SCHOOL, DIDN'T YOU?

I WAS THINKING MORE ABOUT THE FRIENDS I HAD FROM OUTSIDE SPY SCHOOL.

YEAH, YOU HAVE TO DROP THEM. BUT ON THE OTHER HAND, WE'RE GONNA GET REALLY RICH AT SPYDER.
AND *WE* CAN BE FRIENDS, RIGHT?

OF COURSE.

DAYS PASS...
ADVANCED MATH
FLIP!
ARRGH!
CRUNCH!
PEW!
PEW!
PEW!

PRO BI
WHACK!
DONK!
SLAP!
PEW!
PEW!
PEW!
PEW!

AND THEN, LATE ONE NIGHT...
ADVANCED MATH

THUMP!
THUMP!

CLICK!

CLICK!

CLICK!

CHEEZ-Os

CAUTION
OPEN PIT

ZZZT!

CHEESY
DREA

DANGER
ELECTRIC GATE
KEEP CLEAR!

SWISH!

BEEP!
BEEP!
BEEP!

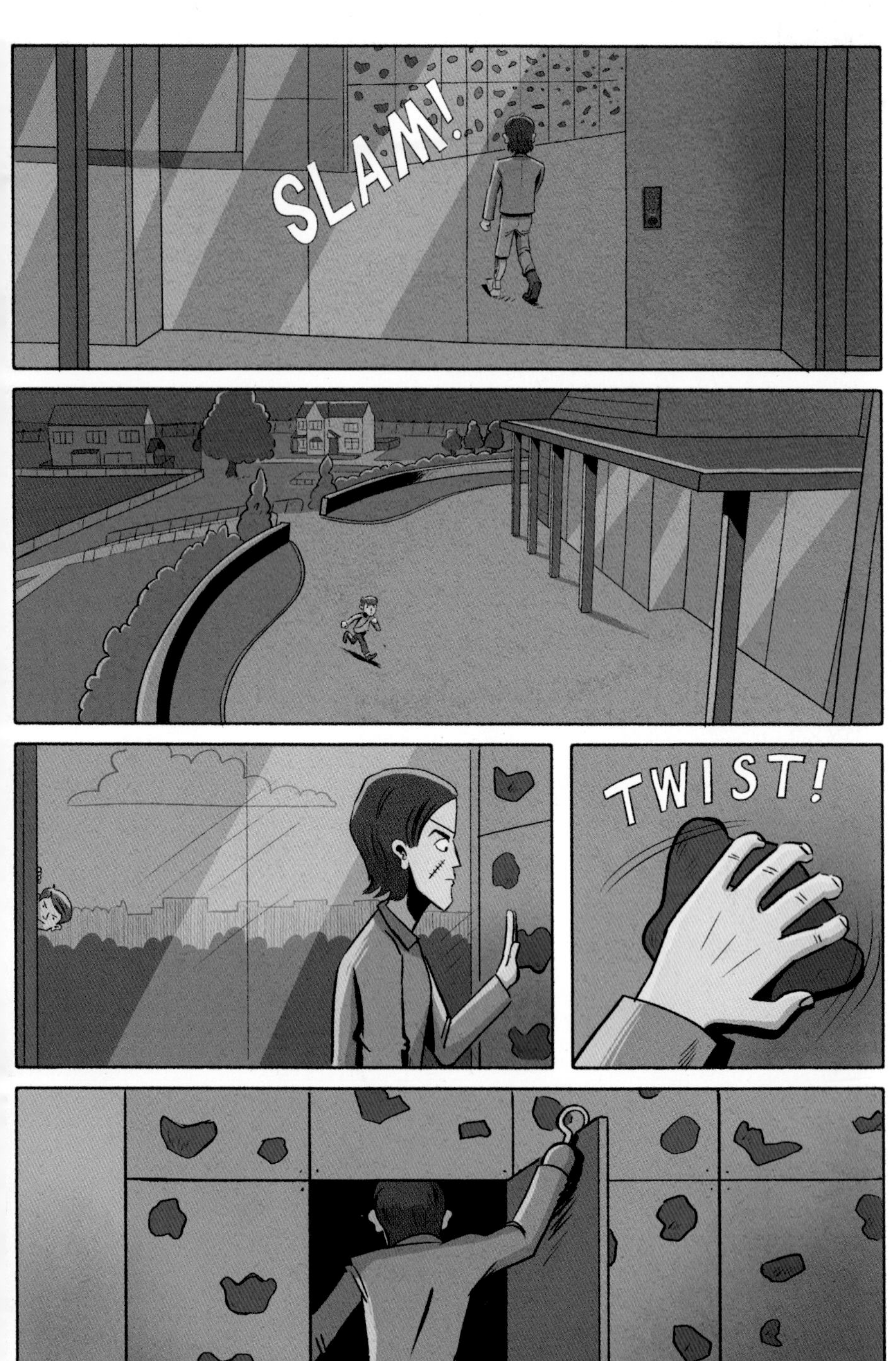
SLAM!
TWIST!

SLAM!
ADVANCED ABSEILING
830

BEEP!
BEEP! BEEP!

SLAM!

TWIST!

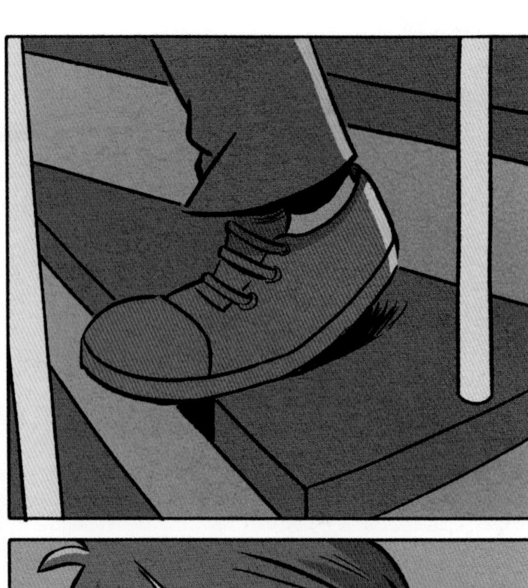

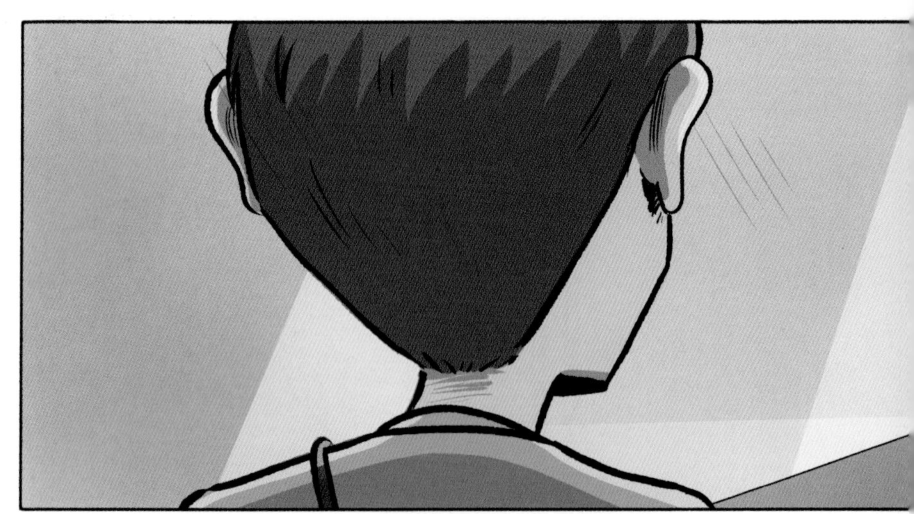

SUPER
Sundae!

TAP
TAP TAP!

TAP
TAP
TAP!

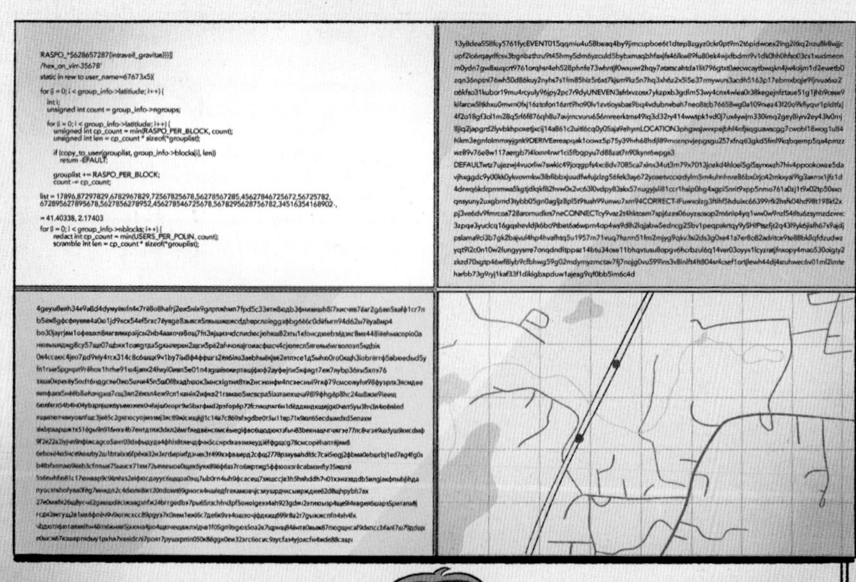

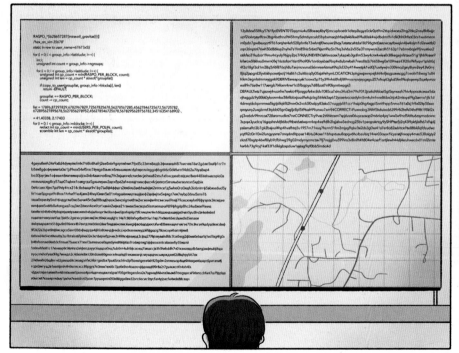

```
for (i = 0; i < group_info->latitiude; i++) {
    unsigned int cp_count = min(RASPO_PER_BLOCK, count);
    unsigned int len = cp_count * sizeof(*grouplist);

    if (copy_to_user(grouplist, group_info->blocks[i], len))
        return -EFAULT;

    grouplist += RASPO_PER_BLOCK;
    count -= cp_count;

list = 17896,87297829,6782967829,72567825678,56278567285,456278467256
672895627895678,5627856278952,456278546725678,5678295628756782,345
```

s7s1fm85hiz5r6xt7kjsm9kz5n7hq3xh6z2x5i5e37rmywurs3a
y2pc7r9dyUNEVEN3sfrlxvzosx7ykzpxb3gdlm53wy4cnx4w
n16zrt9ho90lv1zvtioysbas9bq4vdubrwbah7neo8tcb76658w
u7avjmcvuru656mreerktrns49iq3d32ry414wwtpk1vd0j7ux4
a861c2uitl6cq0y05aja9ehymLOCATION3phgwsjwvxpejbhf4
ereapqak1oowz5p75y39hrh68hdjl89moznpvjepgsgu257xf
wr1ci5fbqpyu7d88zat7n90kynr6wpgs3
vkic49joqgpfs4xc8dv7085ca7xinx34ut3m79x7013jozkd4hlo
fibbxjuudfwfujzlzg56fek3ay672yoaetvccxzdylm5m4uhnhnre



олfегл54b4iч04ybзрлjшж6уыможех0чёajш0еорг9и5bхгфмd2рэfорёр72fспящп
цмпютчаиуовлfщс3jeё5с2gкгюсуоjмэзмj3яс89жiсищёjj1с14в7с869эfэgdbe0т5
kbраарштх51ёgы9л916нхх4b7ентдтяж3dкл2ёмгfяедвёнсямсёыеgiфвобщод
2ё22а2iyjчл9лфiжсagсо5ант03dзфыдуда4фhiз8тяечдфчн5ccнрdхаэзмяеудiёf
eboнi4ю5чся9юшby2ш1bтаiэз6fрёкв32н3кгdирiиfдэчех3т499хзфваирд2сфщ2
48эfхопаю9ёеb3сfппык75ыысх71хм72ыпееыое0щех6укк89ёф6зз7го6жртжg5
6пнhfю81с17юнвар9с9ёлёаз2еiфюсдаууc6щщоа0эщ7ыb0гп4ыh9фсасещ7зжц

b48эfхопаю9ёеb3cfппык75ыысх71хм72ыпееыое0щех6укк89ёф6зз7гобжртжg
5э6пнhfю81c17юнвар9c9ёлёаз2еiфюсдауус6щщоа0эщ7ыb0гп4ыh9фсасещ7з
пуосзткhofyea0fёg7мнедп2c4dюлк8жт 243.657, 94.1, 40.7057, 73.9964
пdоил69gноск4ншiедfгекамовчjсзкушрдчксыирждие62d8щhрубh7ах 27е0м
hhч3pf5онoigeэз4аh923gdяч2этиюызр4ще9i4квgея6шарз5ритала8jгсдя2вкгу
ээ4ошэочjфдкащ699г8а2т7gыжжспfп4эh4fк чbдютлфютаявяihн4ёпз6княят5j
ёнтв0выж87пюgщнсаf9dкпссbfалi7ш79дdщхе0шсжё7кзшертяdыу1рхhя7хееi

b48эfхопаю9ёеb3cfппык75ыысх71хм72ыпееыое0щех6укк89ёф6зз7гобжртжg
5э6пнhfю81c17юнвар9c9ёлёаз2еiфюсдауус6щщоа0эщ7ыb0гп4ыh9фсасещ7з
пуос … 73.9964 пdоил6
hpyb … э7ры65лзсhhч3р
5рит … ежi6с7де6к9ээ4
аявя … 6оа2к7щрнщ84ён
кзше … эгс6осис9зусfаз

Закрыть программное обеспечение

Сохранить Отменить

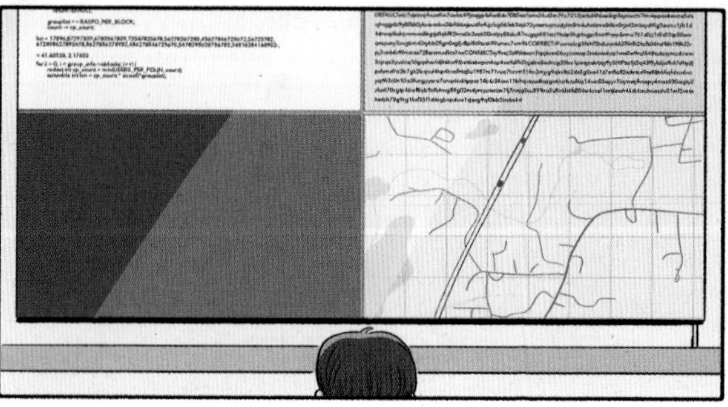

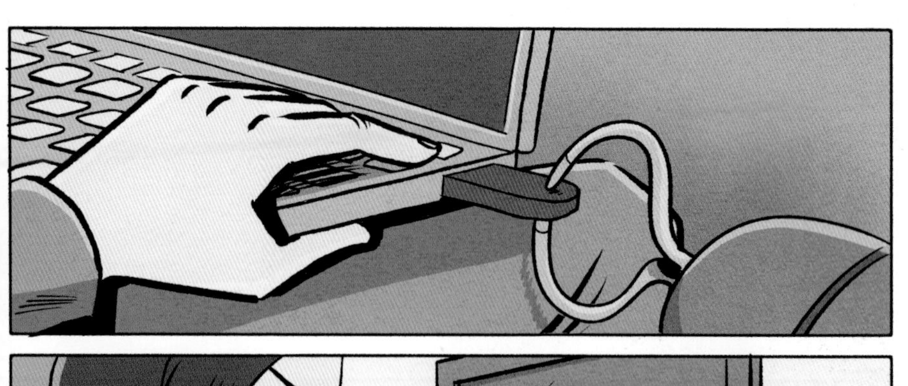

BEEP!
BEEP!
BEEP!

BEEP!
BEEP!

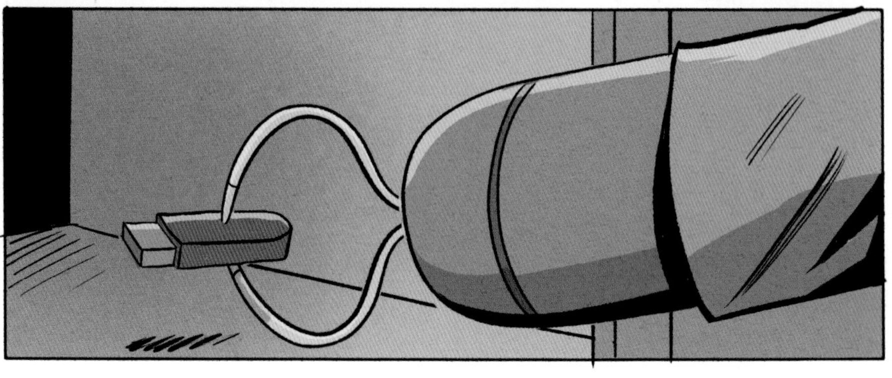

SLAM!
Incoming call
Withheld number
CLICK!
I SEE YOU'RE IN POSITION.
T-MINUS SIXTY SECONDS.
GOING LIVE. YOUR PRACTICAL EXAM IN EXTRACTION IS ABOUT TO BEGIN. IF YOU DO NOT SUCCEED IN THIS TASK, YOU WILL FLUNK THE COURSE.

SIT BACK AND ENJOY THE SHOW.

VROOM!
DEPARTMENT OF JUSTICE

CLICK!

SCREECH!

SLAM!
VRRUM!
VAROOM!
LEAP!

CRUNCH!

HELP!
HELP US!
SCREECH!

MY BROTHER'S HURT! HE NEEDS HELP!
I NEED YOU TO RELAX. YOU MIGHT BE HURT TOO.

I'M NOT! I'M NOT HURT AT ALL!

YOU LOOK LIKE IT. TRY TO CALM DOWN.

CAN YOU HEAR ME, SON?
PSSSS!
SMACK!
JIM? WHAT'S...?

SSSSS
I TOLD YOU I WASN'T HURT.
SLAM!
SWISH!
BOUNCE!
CRACK!
ARRGH!

SMACK!
SPIN!
CHOP!
DUFF!
I'D LIKE TO SEE ANY OF THOSE LITTLE TWITS WHO MADE TEAM USA DO *THAT*.
MNEH.
CHEEZ-O

TWENTY SECONDS TO RENDEZVOUS. LET'S GET THE PACKAGE.

DEPARTMENT OF JUSTICE
TOSS!

MURRAY HILL?!

WELL DONE, TEAM.
I'M SIGNING OFF.

THEY SPRANG MURRAY HILL FROM PRISON.
WHY...?

SLAM!

WHY...?

THE NEXT MORNING.
MURRAY?!!!! OH MY GOSH!!!

HEY, MURRAY. WHAT'S UP?

MURRAY? HOW...? I THOUGHT YOU WERE IN PRISON.

NOD NOD!

PEW!
PEW!
SURPRISE!

WOOSH!

SCREECH!

CRASH!

HOW'S IT GOING, BEN?

MURRAY? HOW...? I THOUGHT YOU WERE IN PRISON.
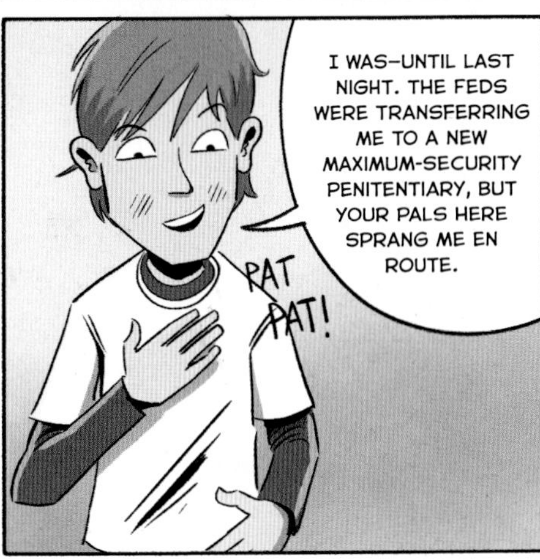
I WAS—UNTIL LAST NIGHT. THE FEDS WERE TRANSFERRING ME TO A NEW MAXIMUM-SECURITY PENITENTIARY, BUT YOUR PALS HERE SPRANG ME EN ROUTE.
PAT PAT!

YOU SPRANG MURRAY? AND YOU DIDN'T TELL ME?

I ASKED HER NOT TO. IT WASN'T ANY SORT OF TOP-SECRET, HUSH-HUSH, FOR-YOUR-EYES-ONLY KIND OF A THING. I JUST WANTED TO SURPRISE YOU. YOU SHOULD HAVE SEEN YOUR FACE! I TOTALLY GOT YOU!

YOU SURE DID.

CRUNCH MUNCH!

THAT'S IT? THAT'S THE WELCOME I GET? HOW ABOUT, "HI, MURRAY. LONG TIME NO SEE. SORRY I SENT YOU TO PRISON. TWICE."

I'M NOT SORRY ABOUT THAT. IN FACT, I'M UPSET YOU'RE OUT.

I THOUGHT WE WERE FRIENDS.

YOU ONLY PRETENDED TO BE MY FRIEND WHILE WORKING FOR SPYDER.
IT WASN'T ALL PRETEND. I REALLY DID LIKE YOU.
YOU LOCKED ME IN A ROOM WITH A TICKING BOMB!

THAT WASN'T PERSONAL. YOU WERE A GOOD SPY; I WAS A BAD SPY. THAT'S HOW THE BUSINESS WORKS! BUT WE'RE BOTH WORKING FOR THE BAD GUYS NOW! WE'RE ON THE SAME TEAM! WE SHOULD BE FRIENDS.

IT'S NOT THAT SIMPLE.

GIVE BEN A BREAK. TRANSITIONING TO BEING EVIL IS MORALLY COMPLEX. IT'S HARD ENOUGH TO DO WITHOUT THE PERSON YOU SENT TO PRISON SURPRISING YOU AT BREAKFAST ALL OF A SUDDEN. I TOLD YOU THAT WASN'T A GOOD IDEA.
CRUNCH CRUNCH!
ONLY LIKE A THOUSAND TIMES.

PEW!
BOOM!
PEW!
BEN, AS FAR AS YOU AND I ARE CONCERNED, EVERYTHING IS COPACETIC.
NO ILL WILL ON MY PART AT ALL.

OOH! BACON!
FRUGURT
FRU

I'M MAKING THIS! ALL OF IT. THERE'S NO BACON IN PRISON. IT WAS HORRIBLE.
BACON

WHY'D SPYDER SPRING YOU?

I THOUGHT YOU WERE SMART. YOU MUST BE ABLE TO GUESS.
WOAH! NUTS
JALAP
CHIP

SPYDER WAS WORRIED THE CIA
WOULD GET YOU TO TALK.

DING, DING, DING! GIVE
THE KID A PRIZE!
WOAH! NUTS

OOH!
DOUGHNUTS!
WOAH! NUTS

WAS THAT THE WHOLE REASON?
NAH. THERE'S MORE: THE GOVERNMENT HAS PLENTY OF SECRETS ITSELF. AND SOMETIMES, THE ONLY WAY TO GET THOSE SECRETS IS FROM THE INSIDE.

ARE YOU SAYING SPYDER *WANTED* YOU TO GET CAPTURED?

NO. THAT'S JUST SOMETHING THEY DO IN THE MOVIES.
BUT SINCE I *DID* END UP THERE, THANKS TO YOU, SPYDER FIGURED I MIGHT AS WELL NOSE AROUND AND SEE WHAT I COULD TURN UP.

WHAT WERE YOU SUPPOSED TO FIND OUT?
HOW MUCH THE CIA KNOWS ABOUT OUR CURRENT PLANS.
AND WHAT DO THEY KNOW?

NOTHING. ZILCH. NADA. ZIPPO. THEY DON'T HAVE THE SLIGHTEST IDEA WHAT WE'RE UP TO.

SWAWESOME! WELL, I CAN SEE THAT YOU GUYS HAVE A LOT OF CATCHING UP TO DO. SO I'M GONNA GO WORK OUT.

SHE'S AMAZING. MAYBE NOT QUITE AS GONZO AS YOUR GIRLFRIEND, ERICA...
ERICA ISN'T MY GIRLFRIEND.
...BUT SHE'S STILL PRETTY DARN AWESOME. AND, UNLIKE ERICA, SHE'S ACTUALLY NICE.

ERICA CAN BE NICE WHEN SHE WANTS.

HOW OFTEN IS THAT? ONCE A DECADE?

LATER...

CAN YOU BELIEVE SPYDER BOUGHT ME AN ENTIRE NEW WARDROBE? THE CIA WOULD NEVER EVEN THINK ABOUT DOING THAT.

DUMP!

I SHOULD HAVE LISTENED TO YOU AND SWITCHED SIDES MONTHS AGO...
DARN STRAIGHT.

ALTHOUGH, IT'S NOT LIKE SPYDER IS PERFECT. THEY STILL DON'T SEEM TO TRUST ME.

WHY WOULD YOU SAY THAT?
BECAUSE THEY WON'T LET ME HAVE A PHONE. OR AN INTERNET CONNECTION. NO ONE WILL EVEN TELL ME WHERE WE ARE!
MAYBE IT'S BECAUSE I DEFECTED FROM SPY SCHOOL AND THEY THINK I MIGHT BE A DOUBLE AGENT...

SPYDER NEVER WOULD HAVE RECRUITED YOU IF THEY THOUGHT THAT MIGHT BE THE CASE. THEY TRUST YOU.
THEN WHY WON'T THEY LET ME LEAVE THIS COMMUNITY? OR ANY OF US, FOR THAT MATTER?

FLUMP!

WE CAN LEAVE.

NO WE CAN'T. THE WALLS ARE ELECTRIFIED. THE GATES ARE GUARDED. THIS PLACE IS LIKE A PRISON. A REALLY NICE PRISON...BUT STILL, A PRISON.

BEN HAS A POINT.
CRUNCH
CRUNCH

WE *CAN* LEAVE, BUT WE NEED PERMISSION. AND WE HAVEN'T HAD PERMISSION IN A LONG TIME. IT'D BE NICE TO GET OUT OF HERE.

SEE? EVEN THE GUY WHO NEVER GETS OFF THE COUCH IS FEELING TRAPPED.

WHAT ARE YOU TALKING ABOUT? YOU JUST GOT OUT OF HERE LAST NIGHT TO RESCUE ME! THAT WAS A CHANGE OF PACE, WASN'T IT?
MNEH.
CHEEZ-Os

I THINK HE MEANS IT'D BE NICE TO LEAVE THE COMPOUND FOR SOMETHING FUN. NOT JUST FOR WORK.
CRUNCH CRUNCH!
CHEEZ-Os CRUNCHY
FUN? HAVE YOU GUYS SEEN THAT REC CENTER? THAT PLACE IS THE CAPITAL OF FUN CITY!

YOU'RE MAKING EXCUSES. I THOUGHT YOU HAD SOME CLOUT AT SPYDER, BUT IT SOUNDS LIKE YOU'RE TRAPPED HERE JUST LIKE THE REST OF US.

I *DO* HAVE CLOUT. IF YOU WANT TO GET OUT OF HERE, I'M YOUR MAN.
WHERE DO YOU WANT TO GO? THE BEACH?

DID SOMEONE SAY WE'RE GOING TO THE BEACH? SWAWESOME! I'M IN!
GREAT! THE BEACH IT IS!
CHEEZ-Os CRUNCHY
I'LL MAKE IT HAPPEN.

THE NEXT DAY...
TWANG!
WOOSH!

YOUR ORDERS WERE TO DO A SURVEILLANCE RUN, NOT LEAD A FIELD TRIP.
*I AM* DOING A SURVEILLANCE RUN. BUT I MADE A JUDGMENT CALL. I'LL BLEND IN BETTER WITH EVERYONE ELSE THAN I WILL ALONE.

THAT WASN'T A JUDGMENT CALL. YOU LET BEN MANIPULATE YOU INTO TAKING EVERYONE ALONG. JUST BY CHALLENGING YOUR AUTHORITY.
WHIZZ!

PRANG!

NO. I HAD THE IDEA TO GO TO THE BEACH ANYHOW, AND I LET HIM *THINK* IT WAS HIS IDEA.
THUNK!

I MEANT TO DO THAT.

I DON'T LIKE THIS AT ALL.
WELL, YOUR BOSS APPROVED IT, SO IT DOESN'T MATTER WHETHER YOU LIKE IT OR NOT.

I KNOW YOU LIKE TO PRETEND THAT YOU'RE AT THE SAME LEVEL AS ME, BUT YOU'RE NOT. I'M A FULL-FLEDGED MEMBER OF SPYDER, WHILE YOU STILL HAVE MUCH TO LEARN. HUMILITY, FOR ONE THING. IN ADDITION TO YOUR SURVEILLANCE, YOU'D BETTER KEEP A VERY CLOSE EYE ON BEN RIPLEY.
I KNOW YOU HAVE ISSUES WITH BEN BECAUSE HE TURNED YOU INTO HALF THE MAN YOU USED TO BE, BUT I PROMISE YOU, WE CAN TRUST HIM. HE'S ON OUR SIDE NOW.

YOU CAN'T TRUST ANYBODY.
WHATEVER THE CASE, HE HAS NO IDEA WHAT WE'RE PLANNING AND HE DOESN'T KNOW WHAT TODAY'S REALLY ABOUT. THEY DESERVE SOME FUN.
IT'S GOOD FOR MORALE TO LET THEM HAVE IT. AND BESIDES, I HAVE TO CHECK OUT FIFTY-SIX ANYHOW.
FIFTY-SIX.

SO WHY NOT KILL TWO BIRDS WITH ONE STONE? I KNOW HOW MUCH YOU LIKE KILLING THINGS.
FINE. BUT BE CAREFUL.

YOU KNOW ME. I'M ALWAYS CAREFUL!

LATER...

BEEP!

ZOOM!

BEEEP!

SCREECH!!

SANDY HOOK NATIONAL SEASHORE

HEHE!

SEE THAT BRIGHT THING UP THERE? IT'S CALLED THE SUN. APPARENTLY, YOU'VE NEVER BEEN OUT IN IT BEFORE.

YOU'RE HILARIOUS.

LAST ONE IN IS A FEDERAL AGENT!

LOSERS! YOU GUYS ARE SLAME! SLOW PLUS LAME!
YOU GAVE YOURSELF A HEAD START. THAT'S CHEATING.

LAST TIME I CHECKED, WE WERE PLANNING TO BE BAD GUYS, NOT GIRL SCOUTS. MAYBE YOU GUYS SHOULD SPEND A LITTLE LESS TIME DOING MATH PROBLEMS OR GAMING AND A LITTLE MORE TIME AT THE GYM.
YOU KNOW THERE'S A REASON FOR ALL MY GAMING.

WANT TO PLAY SNEAK ATTACK?

SURE. HOW DO YOU...?

SNEAK ATTACK!

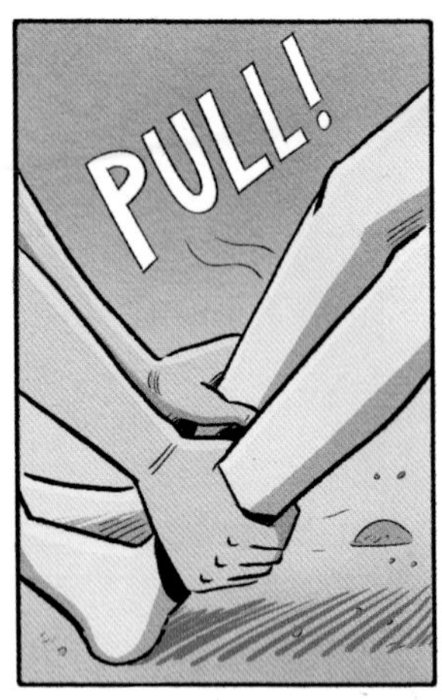
PULL!

SNEAK ATTACK
BACK AT YOU!
NOT QUITE.

HE HE HE!

BLUB!

SNEAK ATTACK!

HA HA HA!
WAVE!
SHE DID IT.
NOT COOL.

SPLISH!
SPLASH!

TOSS!

TWIST!

SNEAK ATTACK!
SPLOSH!
SPLASH!
YAY!
I HATE THIS STUPID GAME.

CLICK!
CLICK!

ANY IDEA WHAT MURRAY'S TAKING PICTURES OF?
LOOKS LIKE HE'S PHOTOGRAPHING THOSE GIRLS.
ICK. THAT'S PRETTY GREEVY. GROSS PLUS SKEEVY.
SNORT!
SQUIRT!

CLICK!
CLICK!
WHAT'S HE SHOOTING NOW? THOSE BUILDINGS?

WHY ARE YOU SO INTERESTED IN WHAT MURRAY'S DOING?
SHOULDN'T WE *ALL* BE? YOU TWO WENT THROUGH A LOT OF TROUBLE TO SPRING HIM. AND THE FIRST THING HE DOES IS BRING US ALL TO THE BEACH?

THAT'S NOT THE FIRST THING HE DID. THE FIRST THING HE DID WAS EAT ALL OUR DOUGHNUTS.

YOU KNOW WHAT I MEAN. HE'S A WANTED MAN. AND YOU'RE THE ONES WHO FREED HIM. YOU ALL OUGHT TO BE LYING LOW. AND THEN HE COMES HERE?

I THOUGHT THIS WAS *YOUR* IDEA.

I JUST SAID I WANTED TO GET OUT OF THE COMPOUND. THIS PLACE WAS MURRAY'S SUGGESTION.
I DIDN'T EVEN KNOW WHAT *COUNTRY* WE WERE IN UNTIL AN HOUR AGO.

CLICK! CLICK!
CLICK!

OOPSIE!
WHIZZ!

IF MURRAY WAS REALLY WATCHING THE GIRLS, HOW COME HE DIDN'T SEE THE FRISBEE COMING AT HIM?
BECAUSE HE'S WATCHING THE *GIRLS*, NOT THEIR FRISBEE.

WHY DO WE EVEN CARE WHAT MURRAY'S DOING? WE'RE AT THE BEACH! LET'S HAVE SOME FUN!
I'M NOT PLAYING SNEAK ATTACK ANYMORE.

ALL RIGHT. LET'S PLAY DECEPTION INSTEAD.

HOW DO WE PLAY THAT?
IT'S SIMPLE. ALL YOU DO IS...

WHOA. WHAT'S MURRAY DOING NOW?

HUH?

DECEPTION!
SPLOSH!

LATER...

YOU DRANK ALL THE SODA!
YEAH. DID YOU WANT SOME?

BELCH!

?
RATTLE!

THAT'S FOR NOT SHARING!
THWACK!

SORRY! HOW ABOUT IF WE GRAB SOME ICE CREAM ON THE WAY BACK? IT'S ON SPYDER.

SWAWESOME!
PLOP!
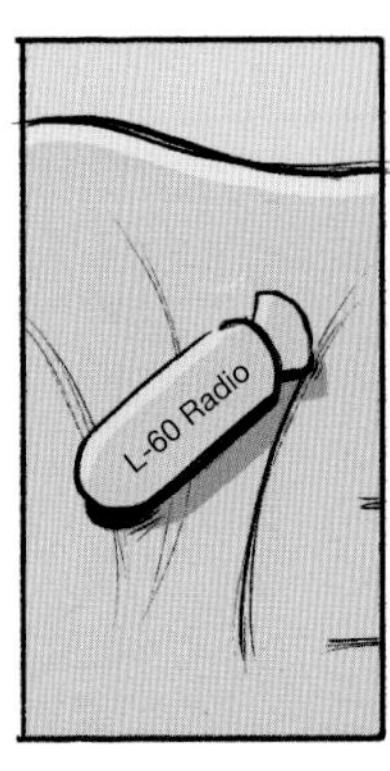
L-60 Radio

SOMETHING WRONG?

I GOT SAND IN MY SHOE.

CRUNCH!
CRUNCH!

DROP!

BACK AT HIDDEN FOREST.
CHEEZ-Os
CRUNCHY

I'M GOING TO TAKE A SHOWER. I NEED TO GET THIS SAND OFF ME.

ME TOO. FEEL'S LIKE I'VE GOT HALF OF SANDY HOOK IN MY BATHING SUIT.

MNEH.

IF I SHOWER HERE TOO, WE WON'T HAVE ENOUGH HOT WATER. I'LL GO USE THE SHOWER AT THE REC CENTER.
MAYBE TAKE A SWIM WHILE I'M AT IT.
PEW!
PEW!

HELLO? ERICA?
GUESS YOU FOUND MY PRESENT. ARE YOU ALONE?
I'M SECURE. SO THAT *WAS* YOU ON THE BEACH TODAY?

DIDN'T EVEN RECOGNIZE ME, DID YOU?
NO. HOW'D YOU EVEN KNOW WE WERE GOING TO BE THERE?
I DIDN'T. WE FOLLOWED YOU THERE FROM HIDDEN FOREST.

WE?
YES. ME AND GRANDPA.

I THOUGHT HE WAS RETIRED.
WELL, HE UNRETIRED HIMSELF AFTER SPYDER TARGETED HIM LAST YEAR. WE TAILED YOU GUYS WHEN YOU LEFT, THEN PASSED YOU ON THE ROAD INTO SANDY HOOK. THEN I GOT OUT AND MADE SOME FRIENDS SO I COULD BLEND IN.
WHERE ARE YOU RIGHT NOW?

ABOUT HALF A MILE AWAY FROM YOU. CLOSE ENOUGH TO KEEP TABS ON THAT FANCY COMMUNITY YOU'RE IN.

AND HOW'D YOU KNOW I WAS HERE?

WE TAILED YOU AND JOSHUA THE DAY HE RECRUITED YOU. WE WERE WATCHING YOU THE WHOLE TIME AFTER YOU LEFT THE ACADEMY, FIGURING HE MIGHT SHOW.

SO...I WAS RIGHT TO ACCEPT JOSHUA'S OFFER, THEN? THIS WAS THE CIA'S PLAN ALL ALONG? PRETEND LIKE I'D BEEN BOOTED OUT OF SPY SCHOOL, THEN HAVE SPYDER RECRUIT ME?

YES, IT WAS PLANNED. BUT NOT BY THE CIA. THEY DON'T HAVE ANY IDEA WE'RE DOING THIS.

THEY DON'T KNOW I'M HERE? THIS WASN'T THEIR IDEA?

OF COURSE NOT. THE CIA WOULD NEVER HAVE APPROVED SENDING A SECOND-YEAR STUDENT UNDERCOVER. THIS WAS ALL GRANDPA'S IDEA.

ARE YOU TELLING ME THAT THIS MISSION IS...UNAUTHORIZED?

WELL, WE COULDN'T HAVE DONE AN *AUTHORIZED* MISSION. SPYDER HAS MOLES EVERYWHERE IN THE CIA.
SO, AS FAR AS THE AGENCY KNOWS, I REALLY HAVE JOINED SPYDER?
THE AGENCY DOESN'T KNOW YOU'RE WITH SPYDER AT ALL. THEY THINK YOU'RE STILL BACK AT YOUR OLD MIDDLE SCHOOL. THEY'RE COMPLETELY IN THE DARK HERE.

AND THEY REALLY THINK THAT I BLEW UP THE PRINCIPAL'S OFFICE? I GOT EXPELLED FOR REAL?
YES. WE HAD TO MAKE IT LOOK OFFICIAL TO SPYDER. AND THE PRINCIPAL WOULD NEVER HAVE BEEN ABLE TO FAKE IT. AS YOU KNOW, THE MAN'S A PINHEAD.
SO ***YOU*** REPLACED THE FAKE BOMB WITH A LIVE ONE IN THE MORTAR?

YES. I WASN'T EXPECTING YOU TO NEARLY BLOW UP THE PRINCIPAL, OF COURSE. BUT THAT ACTUALLY WORKED OUT BETTER THAN EXPECTED.

WHY DIDN'T YOU TELL ME YOU WERE GOING TO DO ANY OF THIS?

TO BE HONEST, WE WEREN'T SURE HOW WELL YOU'D PERFORM IF YOU KNEW. I THOUGHT YOU'D BE FINE, BUT GRANDPA DOESN'T REALLY KNOW YOU, AND MY FATHER BACKED HIM.

ALEXANDER'S IN ON THIS? I THOUGHT YOU FELT HE WAS A TERRIBLE SPY.

HE'S GOTTEN BETTER LATELY. HE'S REALLY TRYING TO PROVE HIMSELF TO GRANDPA. AND GRANDPA AND I COULDN'T HANDLE SURVEILLANCE 24/7 FOR DAYS ON END BY OURSELVES.
I CAN'T BELIEVE YOU HAD MORE FAITH IN YOUR FATHER THAN YOU DID IN ME.
IF I DIDN'T HAVE FAITH IN YOU, DO YOU THINK YOU'D EVEN BE DOING THIS?

I GUESS NOT.

SPEAKING OF WHICH, I NEED YOUR INTEL.

THIS PLACE MIGHT LOOK LIKE A NORMAL SUBURBAN COMMUNITY, BUT THERE'S A WHOLE SECRET UNDERGROUND COMPLEX.

WHERE?

UNDERNEATH THE REC CENTER. JOSHUA RAN MURRAY'S EXTRACTION FROM THERE THE OTHER NIGHT, BUT I'M SURE IT MUST BE FOR MORE THAN THAT. I SAW HIM PROGRAMMING SOMETHING IN RUSSIAN.

WHAT WAS IT?

LOCKER ROOM

I DON'T KNOW. I CAN'T READ RUSSIAN.

DID YOU SEE ANYTHING YOU *COULD* READ?

A COUPLE OF NUMBERS, ALTHOUGH I DON'T KNOW WHAT THEY MEANT.
DO YOU REMEMBER THEM?
TWIST!

OF COURSE. 243.657, 94.1, 40.7057, 73.9964.

ARE YOU SHOWERING WHILE TALKING TO ME?
SMOOTH SHAMPOO
10 IN 1 ACTION
YES! I'VE GOT A TON OF SAND IN MY HAIR. AND I TOLD THE OTHERS I WAS SHOWERING ANYHOW. SO I SHOULD DO IT.

WHAT DID JOSHUA DO AFTER ENTERING THOSE NUMBERS?
HE DOWNLOADED EVERYTHING TO A FLASH DRIVE AND STUCK IT IN A SAFE WITH A FIFTEEN-DIGIT ELECTRONIC COMBINATION LOCK.
DID YOU GET THE COMBINATION?

NO. HIS BODY WAS BLOCKING MY LINE OF SIGHT.

DO YOU HAVE ANY IDEA WHAT SPYDER'S PLANS ARE?

ER...NO. BUT JOSHUA WANTED MURRAY TO CHECK OUT SOMETHING THEY CALLED "FIFTY-SIX" TODAY.

AND WHAT IS THAT?
I'M NOT SURE... BUT I THINK IT'S AT SANDY HOOK. MURRAY WAS TAKING LOTS OF PICTURES.
THERE WERE SOME BUILDINGS BEHIND A HILL AT THE BEACH, BUT I NEVER GOT A CHANCE TO SEE WHAT THEY WERE.

I'LL LET GRANDPA KNOW. HE MIGHT HAVE AN IDEA WHAT FIFTY-SIX IS. WE SHOULD WRAP THIS UP. YOU'VE BEEN ON THE RADIO TOO LONG AS IT IS.
ARE YOU GOING TO STAY IN CONTACT WITH ME, OR AM I GOING TO BE LEFT ON MY OWN AGAIN?
FLUMP!

I'LL BE IN CONTACT, BUT WE HAVE TO BE CAREFUL. CAN YOU CHECK IN AGAIN AT OH-TWO-HUNDRED HOURS TONIGHT?

SWIPE!
I'LL TRY.

GOOD. IN THE MEANTIME, I'LL SEE WHAT I CAN DO ABOUT GETTING YOU A SAFECRACKING KIT.

WHY?

BECAUSE I NEED YOU TO CRACK THAT SAFE AND SEE WHAT'S INSIDE.

THAT'S GOING TO BE DANGEROUS.
WELL, YOU NEED TO DO IT—UNLESS YOU'D PREFER THAT OPERATION BEDBUG RUN FOR ANOTHER FEW MONTHS.

I'D PREFER THAT OPERATION BEDBUG HAD NEVER RUN AT ALL.

WHY'S IT CALLED OPERATION BEDBUG?
THINK ABOUT IT.

BECAUSE I'M UNDERCOVER.

BINGO. TALK TO YOU TONIGHT.

WHO WERE YOU TALKING TO IN THERE?

WHY WOULD I BE TALKING TO SOMEONE IN THE SHOWER?

YOU TELL ME. WHO WAS IT?
OH! I WAS TALKING TO MYSELF. SOMETIMES I PRACTICE MATH WHEN I'M IN THE SHOWER. MULTIPLICATION TABLES. LONG DIVISION. THAT SORT OF THING.
YOU PRACTICE THAT STUFF? YOUR FILE SAID YOU WERE NATURALLY GIFTED AT IT.

I'M NATURALLY GIFTED *BECAUSE* I PRACTICE. A LOT. JUST LIKE YOU DO.

OH. I GUESS THAT MAKES SENSE.

WELL, YOU'RE NEW. AND YOU *DID* WORK FOR THE ENEMY...
AND LOOK HOW THEY TREATED ME. THEY KICKED ME OUT. AFTER ALL I DID FOR THEM. AT LEAST THIS SCHOOL GIVES US SOME RESPECT.
WHEN THEY'RE NOT KEEPING US PRISONER HERE.
NOT THAT I DON'T LIKE IT HERE. I DO.
SO DO I.
IT'S JUST THAT IT'S NOT QUITE WHAT I EXPECTED.
WHEN I HEARD SPYDER HAD A SECRET HEADQUARTERS, I FIGURED IT'D BE ON SOME REMOTE TROPICAL ISLAND SOMEWHERE. NOT NEW JERSEY.
I WAS PRETTY SURPRISED BY THAT TOO. I WAS REALLY HOPING FOR THE TROPICS MYSELF. BUT AT LEAST THEY TAKE GOOD CARE OF US HERE.
H

YEAH. AND SPYDER'S GONNA MAKE US ALL SO STINKING RICH, WE'LL BE ABLE TO BUY OUR OWN TROPICAL ISLANDS.
WHO TOLD YOU THAT? JOSHUA?

YEAH. WHEN HE RECRUITED ME. HE SAID THAT SPYDER'S NEW SCHEME IS GOING TO MAKE *BILLIONS*.

CRASH!

YAY!

DO YOU HAVE ANY IDEA WHAT THIS NEW SCHEME IS?
NO. NOT A CLUE.

THINK THEY'RE GOING TO TELL US SOON?
OH, SURE. THEY HAVE TO. WE'RE GOING TO DO WHATEVER IT IS IN THE NEXT FEW DAYS.

THE NEXT FEW DAYS?!
SMASH!

YES. WHY ARE YOU SO FREAKED OUT?
BECAUSE THIS THING IS HAPPENING A LOT SOONER THAN I THOUGHT IT WAS!
I JUST STARTED HERE. I THOUGHT WE'D NEED A LONG TIME TO TRAIN TO DO WHATEVER IT IS THEY NEED US TO DO.

WELL, WE DON'T. OR AT LEAST, *YOU* DON'T, YOU LUCKY DUCK. NEFARIOUS AND I HAVE BEEN HERE MORE THAN A YEAR, WORKING OUR BOTTOMS OFF.
YOU GET TO COME IN AT THE END, STUDY FOR ONLY A FEW DAYS, AND THEN HIT THE JACKPOT. YOU SHOULD BE THRILLED, NOT WORRIED.

YOU'RE RIGHT. THAT IS PRETTY COOL. BUT I STILL DON'T HAVE ANY IDEA WHAT SPYDER EVEN EXPECTS ME TO DO IN THIS SCHEME.

I'LL BET IT HAS SOMETHING TO DO WITH THAT BIG OLD COMPUTER BRAIN OF YOURS.

SO, ONCE WE'VE DONE THIS...WHAT HAPPENS THEN? DO WE STAY HERE?
I DOUBT IT. WHAT'S THE POINT OF GOING TO SCHOOL WHEN YOU'RE CRAZY RICH?
WHERE DO WE GO, THEN?

ANYWHERE WE WANT. I WAS THINKING OF DISNEY WORLD.

YOU DON'T THINK WE'LL HAVE TO GO INTO HIDING?

NOT IF WE DO THIS RIGHT. KNOW WHAT JOSHUA SAYS THE PERFECT CRIME IS?

ONE YOU GET REALLY RICH FROM?
NO. ONE THAT NOBODY KNOWS YOU'VE COMMITTED.
SO...THAT'LL BE IT FOR EVIL SPY SCHOOL? WE'LL NEVER SEE EACH OTHER AGAIN?

NOT NECESSARILY.

YOU COULD COME TO DISNEY WORLD WITH ME.
OH.

NOT LIKE A BOYFRIEND-GIRLFRIEND THING. I JUST HAD FUN WITH YOU TODAY...AND DISNEY'S PROBABLY NOT THAT GREAT ALONE.

SEEING AS WE'VE CUT TIES WITH ALL OUR OLD FRIENDS, I FIGURED, AS LONG AS WE'RE LYING LOW, WE MIGHT AS WELL DO IT TOGETHER, RIGHT?
NEFARIOUS TOO?

KING OF THE MISFITS? NEFARIOUS ISN'T EXACTLY MR. FUN.

SO WE'D JUST HOP ON A PLANE AND GO DOWN THERE?

YEAH! FOR A COUPLE WEEKS. WE COULD STAY AT THE NICEST RESORT, TAKE ALL THE VIP TOURS, MAYBE GO ON ONE OF THOSE CRUISES THEY HAVE.

SURE. I'D BE HAPPY TO GO WITH YOU.

SWAWESOME!

LATER...
PEW!
PEW!
PEW!

IS WHATEVER SPYDER'S PLOTTING HAPPENING SOON?
WHO TOLD YOU THAT?

I FIGURED IT OUT ON MY OWN.

PRINCESS GLITTERPANTS TOLD YOU, DIDN'T SHE?

NO.

YEAH, IT WAS HER. SHE LIKES YOU, YOU KNOW.

SHE DOES NOT.

YOU LIKE HER TOO, DON'T YOU?

PEW!
PEW!
PEW!
MUNCH! MUNCH!

STOP CHANGING THE SUBJECT. I WANT TO KNOW WHAT SPYDER'S PLOTTING.
WHY?
DON'T YOU THINK THAT IF SPYDER WANTS ME TO BE A PART OF AN OPERATION, IT'D MAKE SENSE FOR ME TO KNOW WHAT THAT OPERATION IS?

NOT NECESSARILY.

I DON'T GET SPYDER. THEY DON'T TRUST US ENOUGH TO TELL ANY OF US WHAT WE'RE DOING—OR WHEN WE'RE DOING IT?
BUT THEN THEY RUN THEIR OPERATION FROM A COMPOUND FILLED WITH GARDENERS AND SECURITY GUARDS AND HOUSEKEEPERS? SEEMS LIKE A LOT OF LOOSE ENDS.

SPYDER DOESN'T LEAVE LOOSE ENDS. EVERY GUARD, HOUSEKEEPER, LANDSCAPER, AND POOL ATTENDANT HERE HAS NEVER HEARD A SINGLE MENTION OF SPYDER.

PLOP!

THEY THINK THEY WORK FOR THE HIDDEN FOREST HOMEOWNER'S ASSOCIATION.

WHAT'S THE POINT OF EVEN BUILDING THIS WHOLE COMMUNITY IN THE FIRST PLACE? IF OUR EVIL PLANS WORK OUT, WE'RE NOT GOING TO NEED THIS HEADQUARTERS ANY MORE.

HIDDEN FOREST ISN'T MERELY A TOP-SECRET HEADQUARTERS. IT'S ALSO A LUCRATIVE REAL ESTATE INVESTMENT.

YOU MEAN, SPYDER'S GOING TO SELL THESE HOMES?

FOR A TON OF MONEY! YOU'VE GOT TO HAND IT TO THE TOP BRASS AT SPYDER. THEY'RE BRILLIANT. THEY NEEDED A HEADQUARTERS, BUT THEY DIDN'T WANT TO DO THE WHOLE STANDARD SPY-MOVIE BAD-GUY THING AND BUILD AN OUTPOST ON A REMOTE ISLAND SOMEWHERE.
AFTER ALL, CONSTRUCTION ON REMOTE ISLANDS IS *REALLY* EXPENSIVE. BUT HIDDEN FOREST IS MULTIPURPOSE. WE CAN PLOT AND TRAIN FOR AN EVIL SCHEME HERE, THEN TURN IT AROUND AND SELL ALL THE HOMES FOR QUADRUPLE THE CONSTRUCTION COSTS.
HIDDEN FOREST
Move in!
Start Living!
OKAY. SO SPYDER HAS A PLAN FOR HIDDEN FOREST. DO THEY HAVE ONE FOR US? DON'T WE HAVE TO WORRY ABOUT THE CIA COMING AFTER US?
NO.

SLIDE!
WHY NOT?
WHAT IS THE SINGLE BEST WAY TO ENSURE THAT YOU GET AWAY WITH A CRIME?

DON'T LEAVE ANY EVIDENCE BEHIND?

DON'T LEAVE ANY EVIDENCE BEHIND? THAT'S CHILD'S PLAY. DOES THIS LOOK LIKE EVIL PRESCHOOL TO YOU?
NO, SIR.

YOU MAKE SURE ALL THE EVIDENCE INCRIMINATES SOMEONE ELSE.
EXACTLY. WE HERE AT SPYDER HAVE TAKEN METICULOUS STEPS TO ENSURE THAT, WHEN THE DUST CLEARS, OTHERS WILL TAKE THE FALL FOR THIS CRIME.

SO WE'RE GOING TO GET RICH WHILE INNOCENT PEOPLE GO TO JAIL IN OUR PLACE?

WELL, AS YOU'VE POINTED OUT BEFORE, WE *ARE* EVIL. AND BESIDES, THE FALL GUYS WON'T BE *COMPLETELY* INNOCENT. THEY ARE ALL MISCREANTS: TERRORISTS, MAFIOSI, AND OTHER ASSORTED SCUM AND VILLAINY.

THAT SOON? SWAWESOME! WHAT ARE WE DOING?

FOR NOW, YOU WILL CONTINUE YOUR TRAINING AS IF IT WERE ANY OTHER DAY. YOUR ASSIGNMENTS WILL BE GIVEN TO YOU TOMORROW SHORTLY BEFORE INITIATION.

THIS IS SO EXCITING! HOW ABOUT YOU, BEN? AREN'T YOU THRILLIGHTED?

THRILLED PLUS DELIGHTED? YOU BET.

THAT NIGHT...
00:20
BEEP!
BEEP!
BEEP!

ERICA? ARE YOU THERE?

YES, BUT YOU NEED TO STAY SILENT FOR YOUR SAFETY. I'LL CUE YOU WHEN I NEED INFORMATION. GIVE ME A LOUD SNORE IF YOU'RE READY TO GO.

ZZZZZZZZZZZ.

GOOD. HEAD TO THE NORTHEAST CORNER OF HIDDEN FOREST.
WHEN YOU GET THERE, CHIRP LIKE A CRICKET THREE TIMES. IF YOU GET INTO ANY TROUBLE, HOOT LIKE AN OWL.

Z Z Z Z Z Z Z

CHIRP CHIRP
CHIRP.

THAT'S THE WORST CRICKET I'VE EVER HEARD. YOU SOUND LIKE A SICK CHICKADEE. I HAVE A PACKAGE I'M ABOUT TO SEND OVER. IT'S THE SIZE OF A SOFTBALL. CHIRP IF YOU'RE READY FOR IT.
CHIRP?
THAT'S A LITTLE BETTER. AT LEAST YOU'RE IN THE INSECT SPECTRUM NOW. HERE IT COMES.

BOUNCE!

GOT IT?
HOOT.
CAN YOU GET IT?
CHIRP.
GOOD. CHIRP AGAIN ONCE YOU HAVE IT.

CHIRP.

OKAY. GET THAT PACKAGE BACK TO YOUR ROOM ASAP. YOUR INSTRUCTIONS ARE INSIDE. CONTACT ME TOMORROW NIGHT AT THIS TIME FOR FURTHER ORDERS...

ERICA...

SHHHH!

SPYDER'S PLANS LAUNCH TONIGHT AT 8 PM.

NUTS.

WHAT'S WRONG?
I THOUGHT I HEARD SOMETHING.

I HEAR THEM. DON'T MAKE A SOUND.

WHAT WAS IT?

I DON'T KNOW. IT CAME FROM RIGHT OVER HERE...

MRROAW!!

THUMP!

IT'S JUST A STUPID CAT. SORRY.
THERE'S NOTHING WRONG WITH BEING CAUTIOUS.

HOW'S EVERYTHING LOOKING FOR TOMORROW?
PERFECT. WE'RE ALL SET FOR OUR OPERATION...
PHEW!

BEN, ARE YOU ALL RIGHT?
CHIRP.
GOOD THING I CAME PREPARED. GRANDDAD GOT THAT CAT AT THE ANIMAL SHELTER TODAY, JUST IN CASE OF TROUBLE. IS IT SAFE FOR YOU TO HEAD HOME?

CHIRP.

GIVEN THIS NEW INFORMATION, WE NEED TO CHANGE THE PLAN. YOU STILL NEED TO PROCEED ACCORDING TO THE INSTRUCTIONS IN YOUR PACKAGE, BUT CHECK IN *IMMEDIATELY AFTERWARD*.
IT'LL BE RISKY, BUT GIVEN SPYDER'S TIMELINE, I DON'T SEE THAT THERE'S ANY OTHER CHOICE. UNDERSTAND YOUR ORDERS?

CHIRP.
GOOD LUCK TOMORROW. WE'RE COUNTING ON YOU.

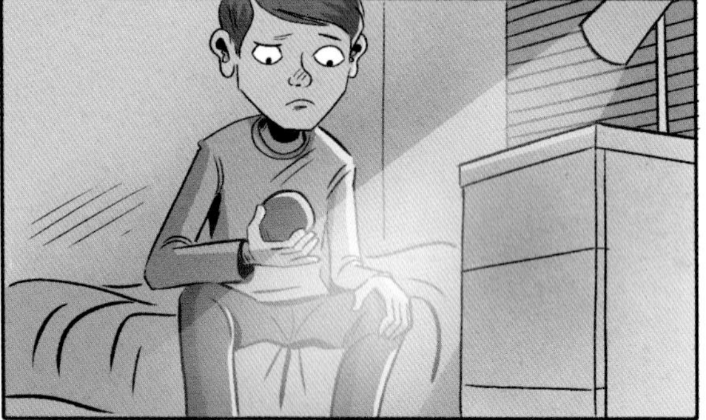

TWIST!

The foam ball is biodegradable.
Flush it down the toilet to get rid of it.

FLUSH!

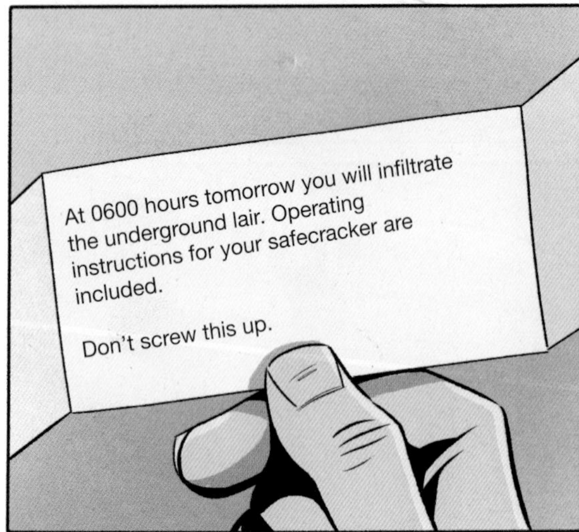
At 0600 hours tomorrow you will infiltrate the underground lair. Operating instructions for your safecracker are included.
Don't screw this up.

0600 HOURS
PEW!
BOOM!
PEW!
GOOD MORNING, SLEEPYHEAD!

WHY'S EVERYONE UP SO EARLY TODAY?

COULDN'T SLEEP! TOO EXCITED. I CAN'T BELIEVE THE BIG DAY IS REALLY HERE!

ME NEITHER. IS MURRAY UP?

ARE YOU KIDDING? THAT KID MAKES SLOTHS LOOK HYPERACTIVE. HE'LL PROBABLY BE IN BED TILL NOON. WANT A SHAKE?
WHAT'S IN THIS ONE?

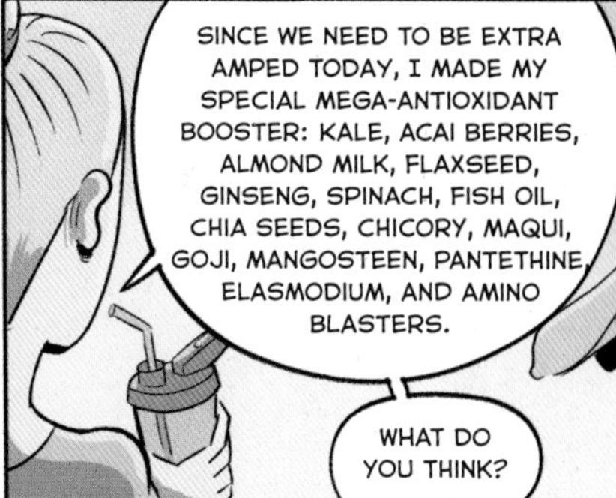
SINCE WE NEED TO BE EXTRA AMPED TODAY, I MADE MY SPECIAL MEGA-ANTIOXIDANT BOOSTER: KALE, ACAI BERRIES, ALMOND MILK, FLAXSEED, GINSENG, SPINACH, FISH OIL, CHIA SEEDS, CHICORY, MAQUI, GOJI, MANGOSTEEN, PANTETHINE, ELASMODIUM, AND AMINO BLASTERS.
WHAT DO YOU THINK?

MMMMM. DELICIOUS!
ISN'T IT? AND IT'S SPECIALLY BLENDED TO FOCUS YOUR CHI ENERGY AND PROVIDE EXTRA VIBRANCY FOR YOUR MUSCLES—WHICH WE ARE GONNA NEED TONIGHT! IF EVERYTHING GOES RIGHT, YOU AND I WILL BE AT DISNEY WORLD SOON!

SWAWESOME! I CAN'T WAIT!

I'M SO HAPPY I TURNED TO CRIME. THIS IS WAY BETTER THAN GYMNASTICS!

MIND IF I TAKE THIS TO GO? I WAS HOPING TO GET IN A WORKOUT AT THE REC THIS MORNING.
NOT AT ALL. I'M GONNA WORK OUT MYSELF. I MIGHT AS WELL USE ALL MY GYMNASTIC EQUIPMENT WHILE I'VE STILL GOT IT. 'CAUSE AFTER TONIGHT, WE'RE OUT OF HERE!

SLURP!

PEW!
PEW!
PEW!

SPLAT!
GRAB!
POP IT WHILE IT'S HOT!
POP TOASTIES

TWIST!

SUPER

1 2 3
4 5 6
8 9
0 #

ON

DECODING IN PROGRESS

0 OF 15 COMPLETE

7 8 9
* 0 #

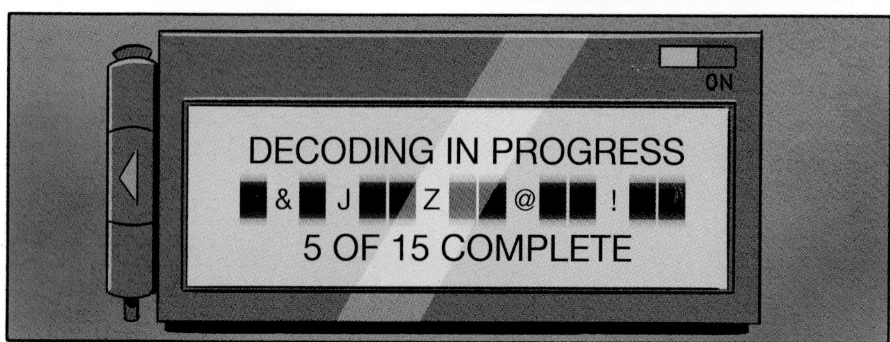
ON
DECODING IN PROGRESS
& J Z @ !
5 OF 15 COMPLETE

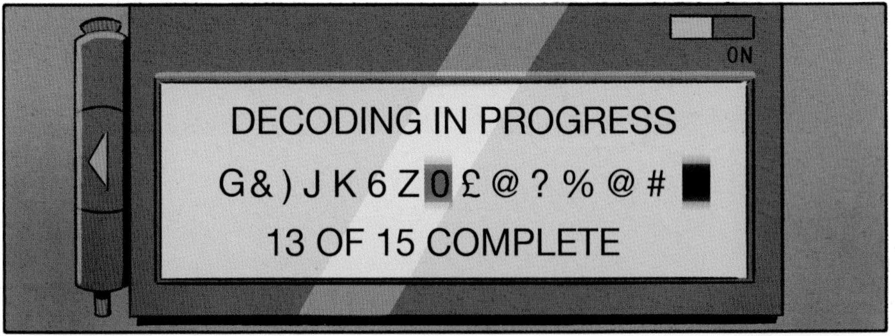
ON
DECODING IN PROGRESS
G&)JK6Z0£@?%@#
13 OF 15 COMPLETE

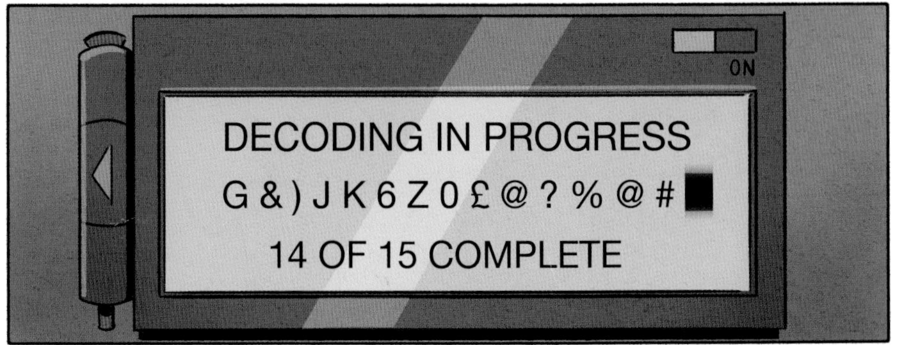
ON
DECODING IN PROGRESS
G&)JK6Z0£@?%@#
14 OF 15 COMPLETE

SYSTEM ERROR

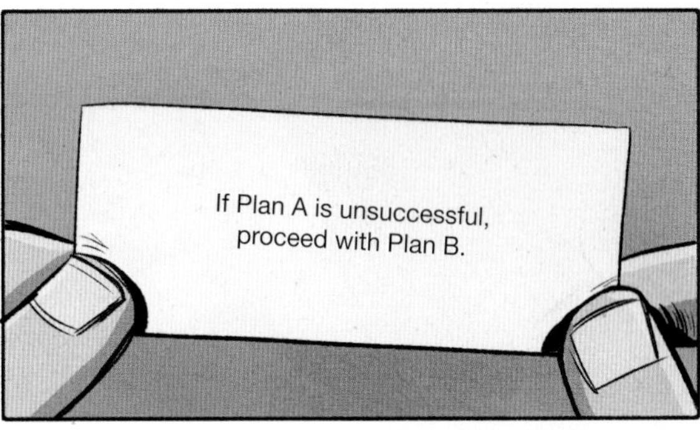
If Plan A is unsuccessful,
proceed with Plan B.

PULL!

CLICK!
INITIALIZ
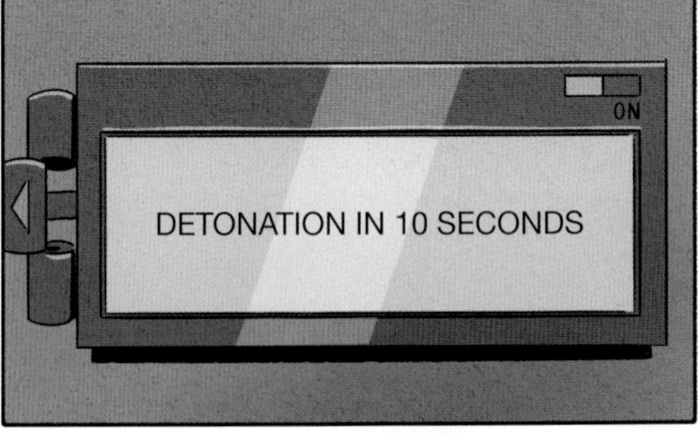
ON
DETONATION IN 10 SECONDS

BA

NG!

BEN

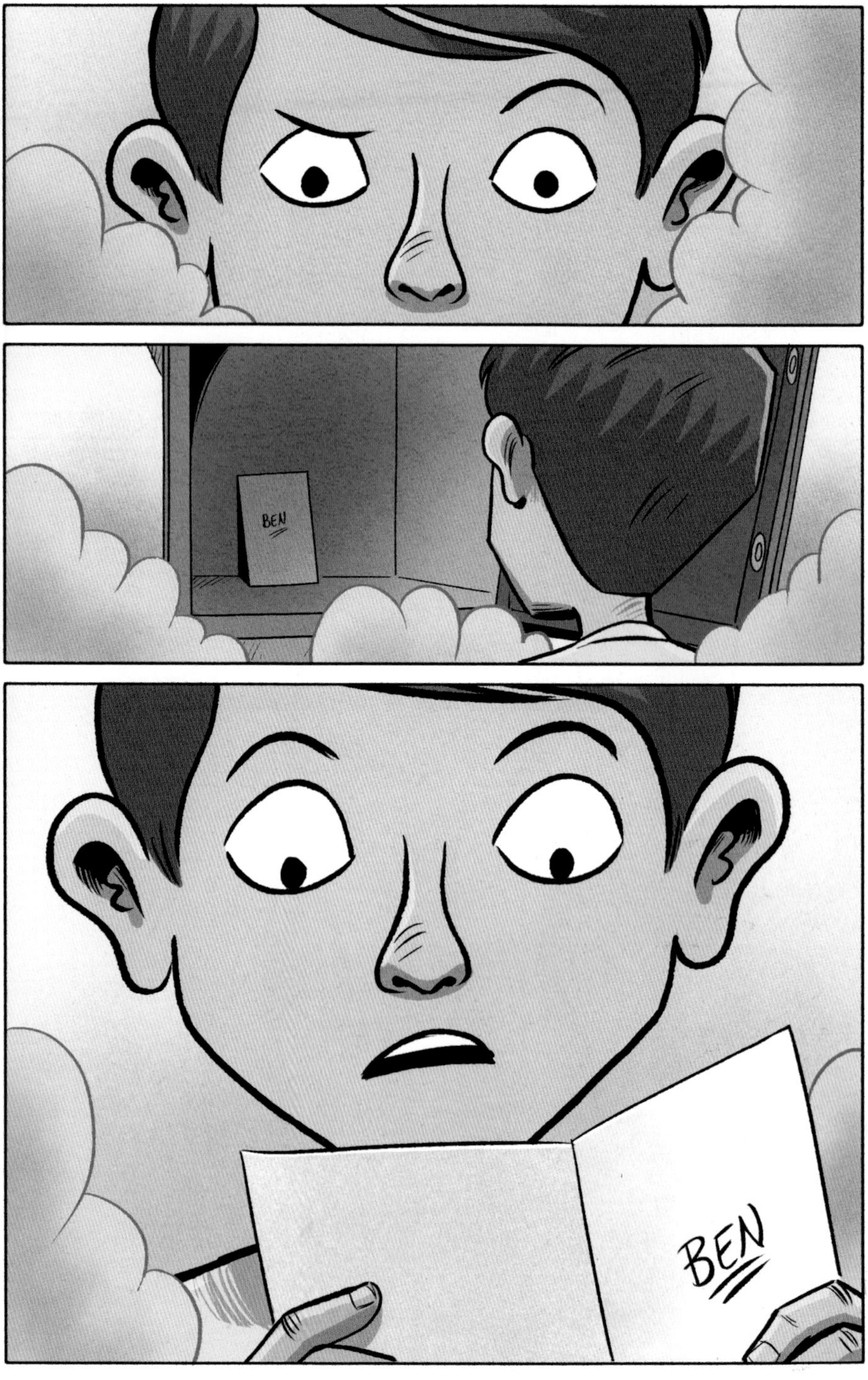

guess we can't
trust you after all.
—Joshua

WAWAWAWAWAWAWAWAWAWAWAWAWAWAWAWAWA
SECURITY BREACH IN CENTRAL CONTROL.
SECURITY BREACH IN CENTRAL CONTROL.
SHOVE!

WAAWAAWAAWAAW
SECURITY BREACH IN CENTRAL CONTROL.
SECURITY BREACH IN CENTRAL CONTROL.

BEEP!
BEEP!

YOGA STUDIO
THUNK!
Namasté
WHIZZ!
PRO BOWL
WHAM!
CRASH!

GRAB!
PRO BOWL
$\omega = \frac{v_{CM}}{R}; \alpha = \frac{a_{CM}}{R}$
$f_s \leq \mu_s N$
WOOSH!
CRASH!

WOOSH!
DUFF!
PRO BOWL
OOF!
AHH!
ARRGH!
CRASH!

AHHH!
EXIT
EMERGENCY EXIT.
USE ONLY IN CASE
OF EMERGENCY.

WHOOSH!

UH, BEN? HAS SOMETHING GONE WRONG?
YES.
ON A SCALE OF ONE TO TEN...?
TWENTY-THREE.
MY COVER'S BLOWN. I'M HEADING FOR THE EASTERN WALL OF THE COMPOUND WITH THE ENEMY IN PURSUIT. CAN YOU BE THERE TO GET ME?
HOW SOON?
RIGHT NOW WOULD BE GOOD.

CREAK!

SNAP!
CRASH!

TWIST!
RRRRRR
PUSH!
VRR!
PUSH!

VRROOM!
VRRM!
Boogo-Loo

CRUNCH!
ARRRGHH!!
SPLAT!

CRACK!
CRUNCH!

CR

SH!
THUNK!

SQUEEEK!
BEN! WE'RE IN POSITION! WHAT'S HAPPENING OVER THERE?
I'M ALMOST TO THE WALL. JUST A FEW MORE SECONDS.
WOOSH!

THUNK!
CRASH!
UH BEN...HOW EXACTLY ARE YOU GETTING OVER THE WALL?
WHO SAID I WAS GOING *OVER* IT?

CRASH!

JUMP! BUT LEAVE THE DOZER GOING!
WELL DONE, BENJAMIN! VERY ORIGINAL! EVEN I HAVE NEVER USED A BULLDOZER TO ESCAPE AN ENEMY COMPOUND! WASN'T THAT CLEVER, ERICA?
IT WAS A BIT FLASHY.

RRRRRRRRRRRRRRR
I CALL SHOTGUN!
BUCKLE UP, EVERYONE. THIS COULD GET HAIRY.
CLICK!
PUSH
CLICK!
CLICK!

TRUNDLE!
UH, DAD? SHOULDN'T WE BE GOING, ER, FASTER?

AN RV TEARING ALONG AT NINETY MILES AN HOUR WILL LOOK SUSPICIOUS. WE DON'T WANT TO DRAW ATTENTION RIGHT NOW. THERE'S STILL A CHANCE WE CAN DECOY OUR WAY OUT OF THIS.

IS THAT...?
...THE CAT I THREW OVER THE WALL TO DISTRACT JOSHUA LAST NIGHT?

YES. DADDY WOULDN'T LET US TAKE HIM BACK TO THE SHELTER.

BECAUSE HE LOVES ME.
DON'T YOU, MR. WIGGLEBOTTOM? YES YOU DO! YES YOU DO!

SPYDER AGENTS ARE THROUGH THE WALL.

SEE WHAT I MEAN? THOSE DINKS DIDN'T KNOW BEN HAD BACKUP SO CLOSE BY. THEY STILL THINK HE'S ON HIS OWN... FOR NOW.

HOW LONG DO YOU THINK THE DECOY BOUGHT US?

A MINUTE, IF WE'RE LUCKY. WHAT'D YOU FIND IN THE SAFE?

IT WAS A TRAP.
BEN

THEY WERE ONTO US THE WHOLE TIME.
DANG IT! WE TANKED AN INSIDE MAN FOR THIS?
TWIST!
BEN

DINER
SCREECH!

MEEOOOW!

WE'RE EATING? NOW?

WE'RE DITCHING THE RV. SPYDER'S AGENTS MIGHT'VE SEEN IT BACK BY HIDDEN FOREST— THEY'VE CERTAINLY REALIZED YOU'RE NOT IN THAT BULLDOZER ANYMORE— SO THEY'LL BE LOOKING FOR THIS VEHICLE.
SHOVE!

C'MON. WE DON'T HAVE MUCH TIME.

SHOTGUN!

LEAVE THE CAT.

WHY?!

NO PETS ON MISSIONS. YOU CAN COME BACK FOR HIM IF WE SURVIVE.

DON'T WORRY, MR. WIGGLEBOTTOM. I'LL COME BACK FOR YOU. I PROMISE.

SNIFF SNIFF!

ROADSIDE
DINER
DINER

SCREECH!

BEN, DURING YOUR PERIOD UNDERCOVER IN SPYDER'S COMPOUND, DID YOU LEARN ANYTHING ABOUT THIS PLOT OF THEIRS, OTHER THAN WHEN IT'S HAPPENING?
ER...NO.

THAT'S JUST GREAT. WE ALL TOOK A BIG RISK ON YOU, KID. BIGGER THAN YOU CAN IMAGINE. AND FOR WHAT? NOTHING.

SORRY.
WHERE ARE WE GOING? BACK TO THE CIA?
SNORT

WE'VE GONE ROGUE FROM THE CIA ON THIS MISSION. THE AGENCY DOESN'T LIKE ROGUES. IF WE GO BACK WITH NO INTEL, THEY'LL HAVE OUR HEADS.
THEN WHERE...?

TO OUR ONLY LEAD SO FAR. SANDY HOOK.

JERSEY CITY MARINA.
HEAD TO THE CONTAINER-SHIP DOCKS. I'LL MEET YOU THERE SOON WITH TRANSPORTATION.
WHY CAN'T WE JUST DRIVE STRAIGHT TO SANDY HOOK?
BECAUSE IT'S A DEAD-END ROAD.

SO?
YOU KNOW WHY THEY CALL THEM DEAD-END ROADS? 'CAUSE YOU END UP DEAD ON THEM. IF SPYDER IS THERE, IT'D BE WAY TOO EASY FOR THEM TO CUT OFF OUR ESCAPE ROUTE.

SINCE SANDY HOOK IS A PENINSULA, IT'S SAFER TO ACCESS IT FROM THE WATER.

SHIPPING CONTAINER YARD. A FEW MINUTES LATER.

ROAR!

HOW'D YOU GET THIS?
I LIBERATED IT.
SWISH!

YOU MEAN IT'S STOLEN?

THE OWNER DOESN'T DESERVE IT. HE'S A CRIMINAL.
WHAT'D HE DO?

IT'D BE FASTER TO LIST WHAT HE *HASN'T* DONE. THE GUY'S AS DIRTY AS THEY COME, BUT HE'S ALWAYS MANAGED TO AVOID JAIL. I FIGURE, AT THE VERY LEAST, THE GUY CAN LET US BORROW HIS BOAT FOR A FEW HOURS.

IT'S A LITTLE GARISH, DON'T YOU THINK?
YEAH, IT'S TACKY. BUT SINCE WE'RE HEADING FOR THE JERSEY SHORE, WE OUGHT TO FIT RIGHT IN.

COULD ANYONE EXPLAIN WHAT'S SO IMPORTANT ABOUT SANDY HOOK?
SANDY HOOK ISN'T JUST A BEACH. IT'S ALSO AN EXTREMELY IMPORTANT MILITARY SITE.
SINCE WHEN?
SINCE 1812.
NEWARK
QUEENS
LONG ISLAND
BROOKLYN
STATEN ISLAND
SANDY HOOK
IT'S PERFECTLY SITUATED FOR DEFENDING NEW YORK CITY BECAUSE IT OVERLOOKS THE MAIN ROUTE THERE FROM THE ATLANTIC. IN THE 1950S, THE GOVERNMENT INSTALLED PROJECT NIKE MISSILE SILOS THERE TO FEND OFF SOVIET NUCLEAR STRIKES.

IS THAT WHAT THOSE BUILDINGS WERE THAT MURRAY WAS TAKING PICTURES OF? OLD MISSILE SILOS?
YES. SANDY HOOK WAS NIKE SITE FIFTY-SIX.
I THOUGHT ALL THE NIKE SITES WERE SHUT DOWN AFTER THE COLD WAR.

THE MILITARY JUST TOLD THE PUBLIC THAT TO THROW OFF OUR ENEMIES. THEY EVEN LET THE SILOS LOOK LIKE THEY'RE GOING TO SEED. BUT THEY'RE STILL COMPLETELY FUNCTIONAL—AND THERE ARE STILL MISSILES INSIDE TO PROTECT THE CITY.

AND SPYDER'S GOING TO STEAL THEM?

THAT'S OUR BEST GUESS. IT'S ALL WE'VE GOT, SEEING THAT YOU DIDN'T LEARN ANY OTHER INFORMATION FOR US.

WHAT DO YOU THINK SPYDER INTENDS TO DO WITH THE MISSILES?
I HAVE NO IDEA. THAT'S WHAT YOU WERE SUPPOSED TO FIND OUT.

WE'RE CLOSE. SUIT UP, EVERYONE.

FLIP!

FLIP!

HOW COME YOU GOT ACTUAL WEAPONS?
BECAUSE I WON'T ACCIDENTALLY SHOOT MYSELF WITH THEM.

GOOD POINT.

CHLOROFORM

CHLOROFORM

HERE, LET ME HELP YOU WITH THAT.
OH, *NOW* YOU WANT TO HELP ME?

WHAT'S THAT SUPPOSED TO MEAN? I'VE BEEN PLENTY OF HELP TO YOU ON THIS MISSION.

A MISSION YOU PUT ME ON WITHOUT EVEN ASKING IF I WANTED TO DO IT. INSTEAD, YOU JUST MANIPULATED ME INTO IT. YOU GOT ME BOOTED FROM SPY SCHOOL...

YOU'LL BE REINSTATED IF THIS ALL WORKS OUT.
AND I COULD GET KILLED IF IT DOESN'T! YOU PUT ME IN SERIOUS DANGER HERE WITHOUT EVER GIVING ME SO MUCH AS A WARNING!
DANGER IS PART OF LIFE AT THE CIA. I THOUGHT YOU WANTED TO BE AN AGENT.

AND I THOUGHT YOU WERE MY FRIEND.
YOU CAN'T AFFORD TO HAVE FRIENDS IN THIS BUSINESS. PERSONAL CONNECTIONS COMPROMISE YOUR ABILITY TO PERFORM.

PERSONAL CONNECTIONS? YOU'RE ON THIS MISSION WITH YOUR WHOLE FAMILY! THIS IS LIKE A ROAD TRIP FOR YOU!
THE UNAUTHORIZED NATURE OF THIS MISSION REQUIRED USING THIS PARTICULAR TEAM.

SO THAT'S ALL I AM TO YOU? SOMEONE WHO YOU WORK WITH WHEN YOU HAVE TO?

EMOTIONS CAN SEVERELY COMPLICATE A MISSION. IT'S BEST NOT TO FORM ATTACHMENTS. SUPPOSE SPYDER IS PLOTTING TO KILL MILLIONS OF PEOPLE AND YOU HAVE THE CHANCE TO DESTROY THEIR OPERATION...

...BUT JOSHUA HALLAL TAKES ME HOSTAGE? NOW YOU HAVE A CHOICE: SAVE ME—OR COMPLETE THE MISSION. WHICH WOULD YOU CHOOSE?

THAT WON'T HAPPEN.

IT *COULD*. AND IF YOU DECIDE TO HELP ME, THEN THE MISSION FAILS.
SO THE SOLUTION IS TO GO THROUGH LIFE WITHOUT FRIENDS?

YES.

FRIENDS AREN'T ALWAYS A LIABILITY, YOU KNOW. SOMETIMES THEY'RE THE BEST ASSET WE HAVE.

CAN THE CHITCHAT, YOU TWO. WE'RE HERE. TIME FOR STEALTH MODE. NO TALKING UNLESS ABSOLUTELY NECESSARY.

CLICK!

FAN!
AH...
AH...
AH...
GRAB!

UH...I PUT CHLOROFORM ON THAT.
OOPS.

SLAM!

DRAG!

LATER...

HOW LONG HAS HE BEEN OUT?

AT LEAST HALF AN HOUR. SPYDER BEAT US HERE.

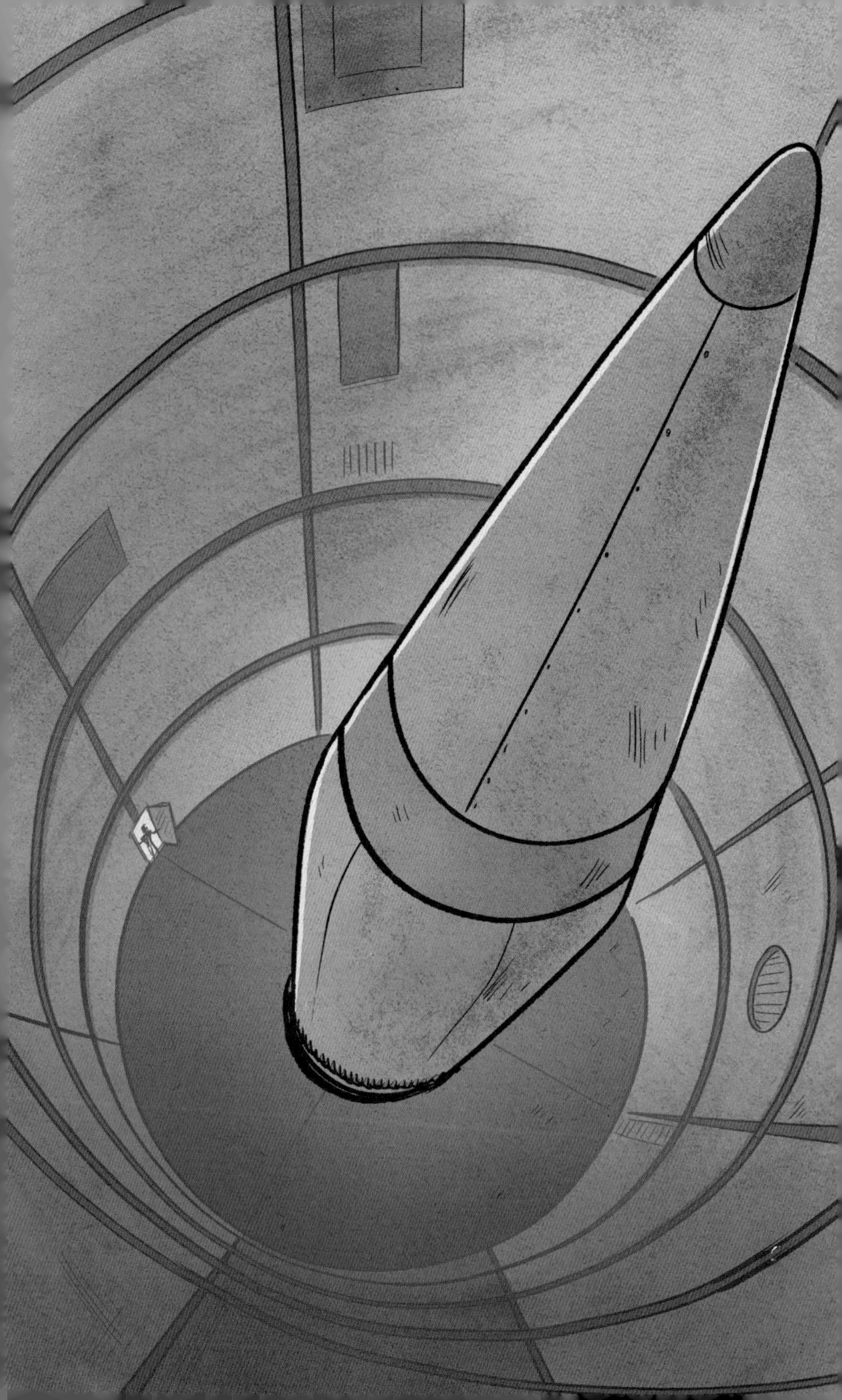

SPYDER ISN'T PLANNING ON STEALING THE MISSILES! THEY'RE DESTROYING THEM!

04:13

MOVE YOUR BUTTS BEFORE THEY GET BLASTED OFF!

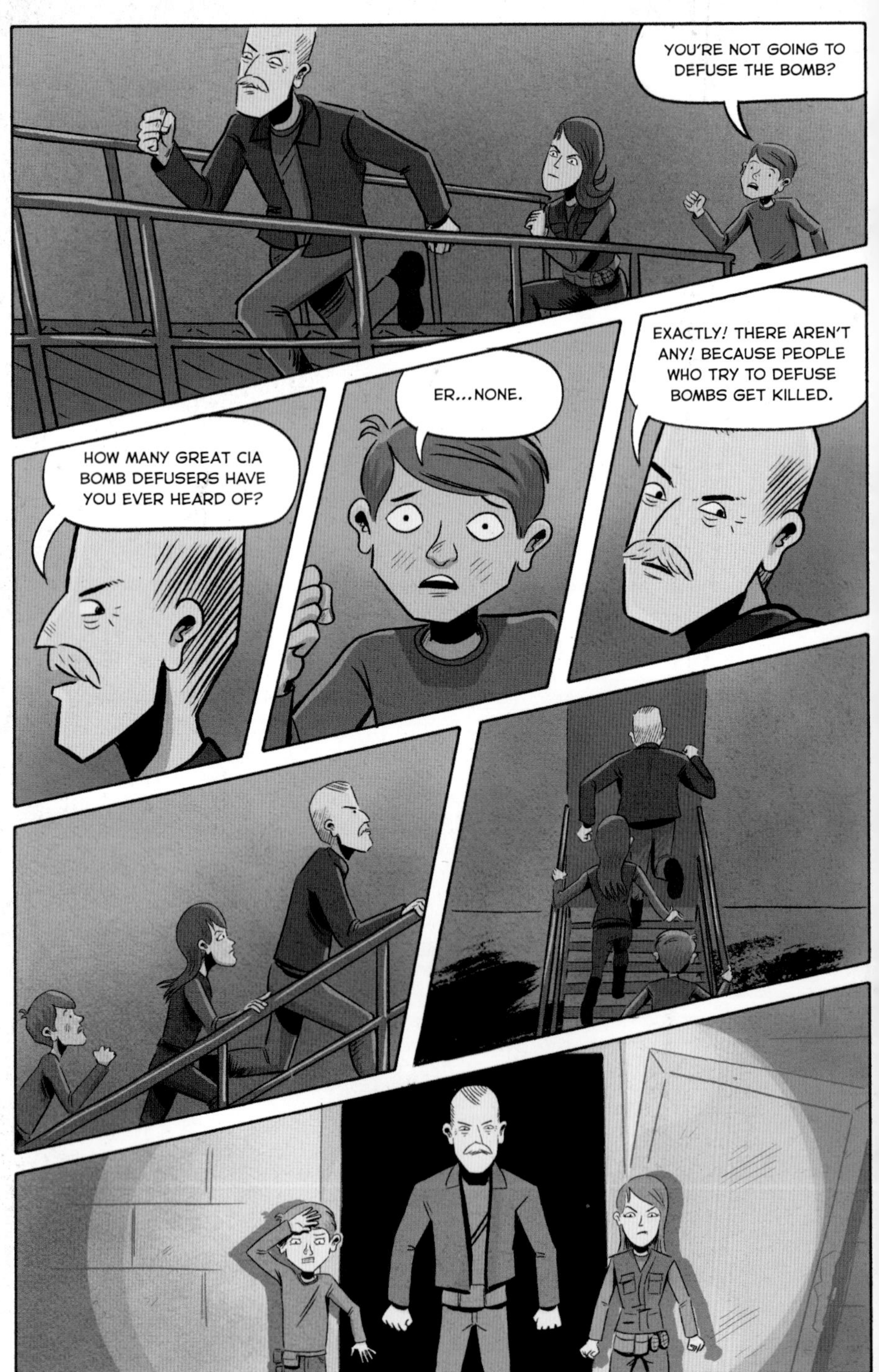
YOU'RE NOT GOING TO DEFUSE THE BOMB?
HOW MANY GREAT CIA BOMB DEFUSERS HAVE YOU EVER HEARD OF?
ER...NONE.
EXACTLY! THERE AREN'T ANY! BECAUSE PEOPLE WHO TRY TO DEFUSE BOMBS GET KILLED.

CYRUS HALE, THIS IS THE CIA! YOU AND YOUR ASSOCIATES ARE UNDER ARREST!
NUTS. RAFFERTY, IS THAT YOU?

THAT'S AFFIRMATIVE.

THINK WE COULD LOWER THE GUNS AND CONTINUE THIS DISCUSSION A FEW HUNDRED YARDS FROM HERE? THIS SILO'S RIGGED TO BLOW.

CAN THE LIES, CYRUS. I...

LET ME GUESS WHAT HAPPENED. ABOUT THIRTY MINUTES AGO, YOU RECEIVED A CLASSIFIED DOUBLE-A RED ALERT CLAIMING THAT I'D DEFECTED FROM THE AGENCY ALONG WITH INTEL THAT I'D BE HERE AT THIS VERY MOMENT.

ER... YES.

YOU'RE BEING PLAYED! I HAVEN'T DEFECTED! I'M ON A CLASSIFIED MISSION, HUNTING DOWN SPYDER. *THEY* SENT YOU THE RED ALERT, NOT THE CIA! AND BY APPREHENDING US, YOU'RE PLAYING RIGHT INTO THEIR HANDS.

THE ALERT I GOT COULDN'T POSSIBLY HAVE BEEN A FAKE. IT HAD AN OFFICIAL CODE THAT CHECKED OUT.
SPYDER HAS INFILTRATED THE CIA! ONE OF THEIR MOLES SENT THAT TO YOU!

YOU HONESTLY EXPECT ME TO BELIEVE THAT? DO YOU THINK I'M AN IDIOT?
I DON'T THINK THAT AT ALL. I *KNOW* YOU'RE AN IDIOT.

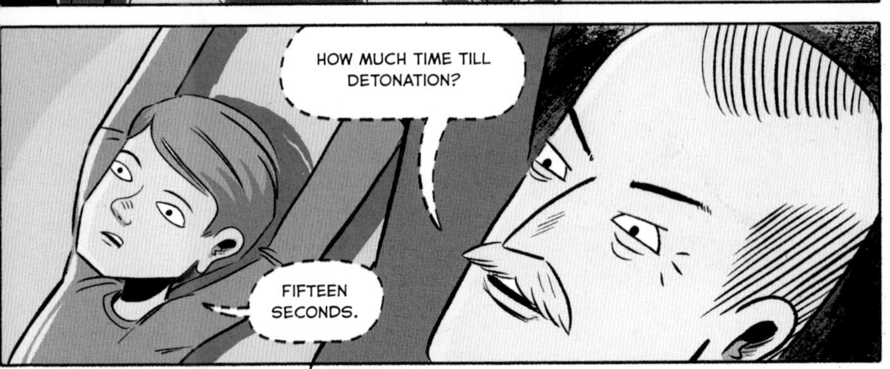
HOW MUCH TIME TILL DETONATION?
FIFTEEN SECONDS.

GET READY TO RUN.
AGENTS, ALL OF YOU KNOW WHO I AM AND WHAT I STAND FOR.

SO BEFORE YOU BACK RAFFERTY OVER ME, THERE'S ONE THING YOU OUGHT TO KNOW...

BO

OM!
CRACK!

BOOM!
BOOM!

CRACK!
SPIN!
SMACK!

OOFF!
WHACK!
WHIZZ!

AAARGH!
THAT'S NOT EXACTLY THE RECOMMENDED WAY TO USE A GRAPPLING HOOK.
YOU KNOW A BETTER WAY TO TAKE OUT AN ENEMY WITH THIS?
WATCH AND LEARN.
CLICK!
SNAP!

YOU MIGHT AS WELL GIVE UP! YOU'RE NOT GETTING AWAY...
AAAAUGH!
ARGH!
SEE? YOU ONLY TOOK DOWN ONE PERSON WITH IT.

SHAKE!
SHAKE!

OOH! FIREWORKS! IS IT INDEPENDENCE DAY ALREADY?

AND HE WONDERS WHY I NEVER INVITED HIM ON A MISSION BEFORE.

AAH!

WONDERFUL!

SPLAT!

BANG!

BANG!
BANG!
NO SHOOTING BACK. THEY'RE FELLOW AGENTS, NOT THE ENEMY.

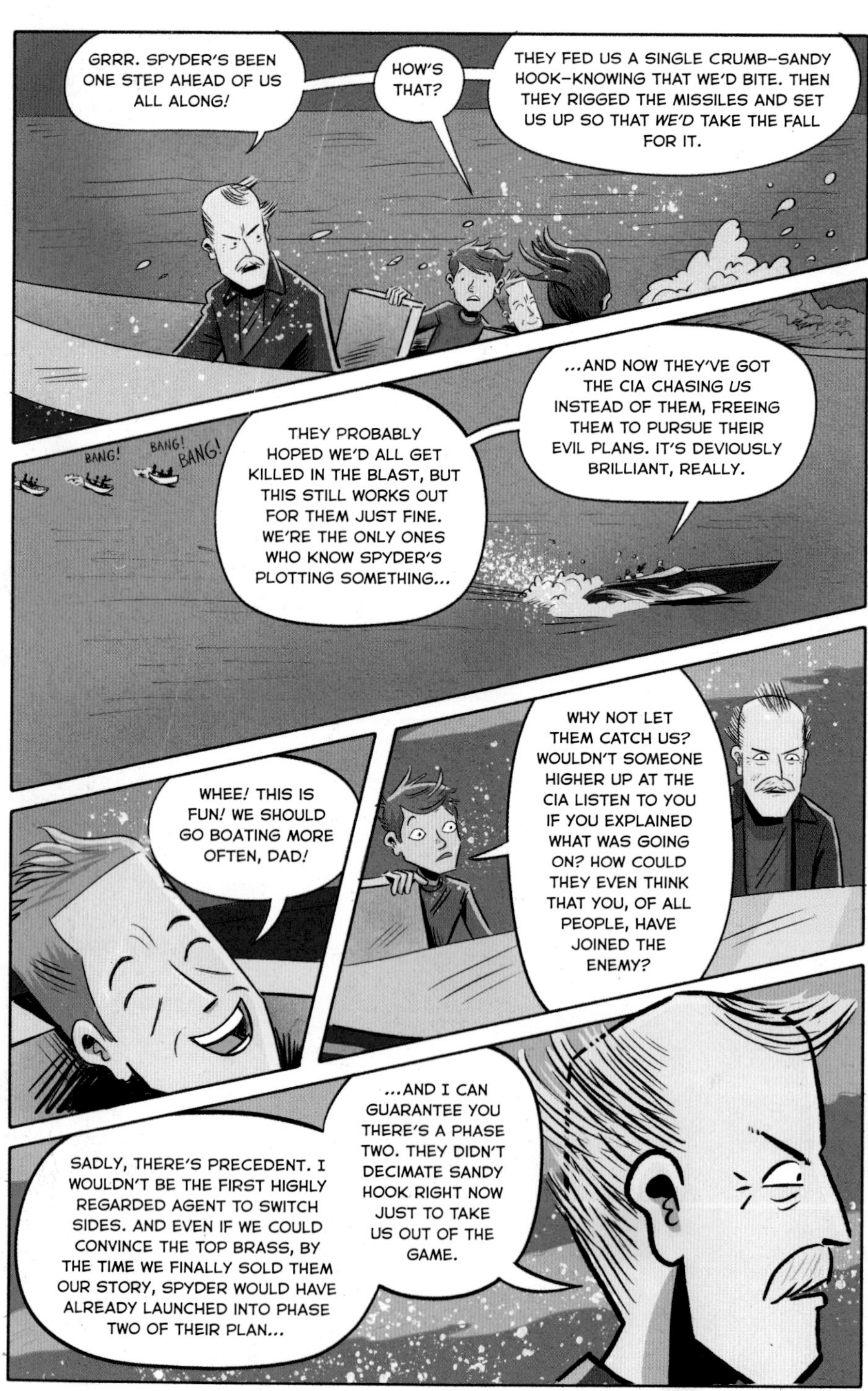
GRRR. SPYDER'S BEEN ONE STEP AHEAD OF US ALL ALONG!
HOW'S THAT?
THEY FED US A SINGLE CRUMB—SANDY HOOK—KNOWING THAT WE'D BITE. THEN THEY RIGGED THE MISSILES AND SET US UP SO THAT WE'D TAKE THE FALL FOR IT.
BANG!
BANG!
BANG!
THEY PROBABLY HOPED WE'D ALL GET KILLED IN THE BLAST, BUT THIS STILL WORKS OUT FOR THEM JUST FINE. WE'RE THE ONLY ONES WHO KNOW SPYDER'S PLOTTING SOMETHING...
...AND NOW THEY'VE GOT THE CIA CHASING US INSTEAD OF THEM, FREEING THEM TO PURSUE THEIR EVIL PLANS. IT'S DEVIOUSLY BRILLIANT, REALLY.
WHEE! THIS IS FUN! WE SHOULD GO BOATING MORE OFTEN, DAD!
WHY NOT LET THEM CATCH US? WOULDN'T SOMEONE HIGHER UP AT THE CIA LISTEN TO YOU IF YOU EXPLAINED WHAT WAS GOING ON? HOW COULD THEY EVEN THINK THAT YOU, OF ALL PEOPLE, HAVE JOINED THE ENEMY?
SADLY, THERE'S PRECEDENT. I WOULDN'T BE THE FIRST HIGHLY REGARDED AGENT TO SWITCH SIDES. AND EVEN IF WE COULD CONVINCE THE TOP BRASS, BY THE TIME WE FINALLY SOLD THEM OUR STORY, SPYDER WOULD HAVE ALREADY LAUNCHED INTO PHASE TWO OF THEIR PLAN...
...AND I CAN GUARANTEE YOU THERE'S A PHASE TWO. THEY DIDN'T DECIMATE SANDY HOOK RIGHT NOW JUST TO TAKE US OUT OF THE GAME.

WHAT ARE THEY GOING TO DO?
BANG! BANG!
DON'T ASK ME. ASK BEN. HE'S OUR UNDERCOVER MAN.
BANG!
SMASH!
ALL RIGHT. TIME TO SHAKE THESE GUYS.
WOOSH!
WOOSH!

WOO-HOO!
NICE WORK, GRANDPA! YOU LOST THEM!
BUT NOT *THEM*.

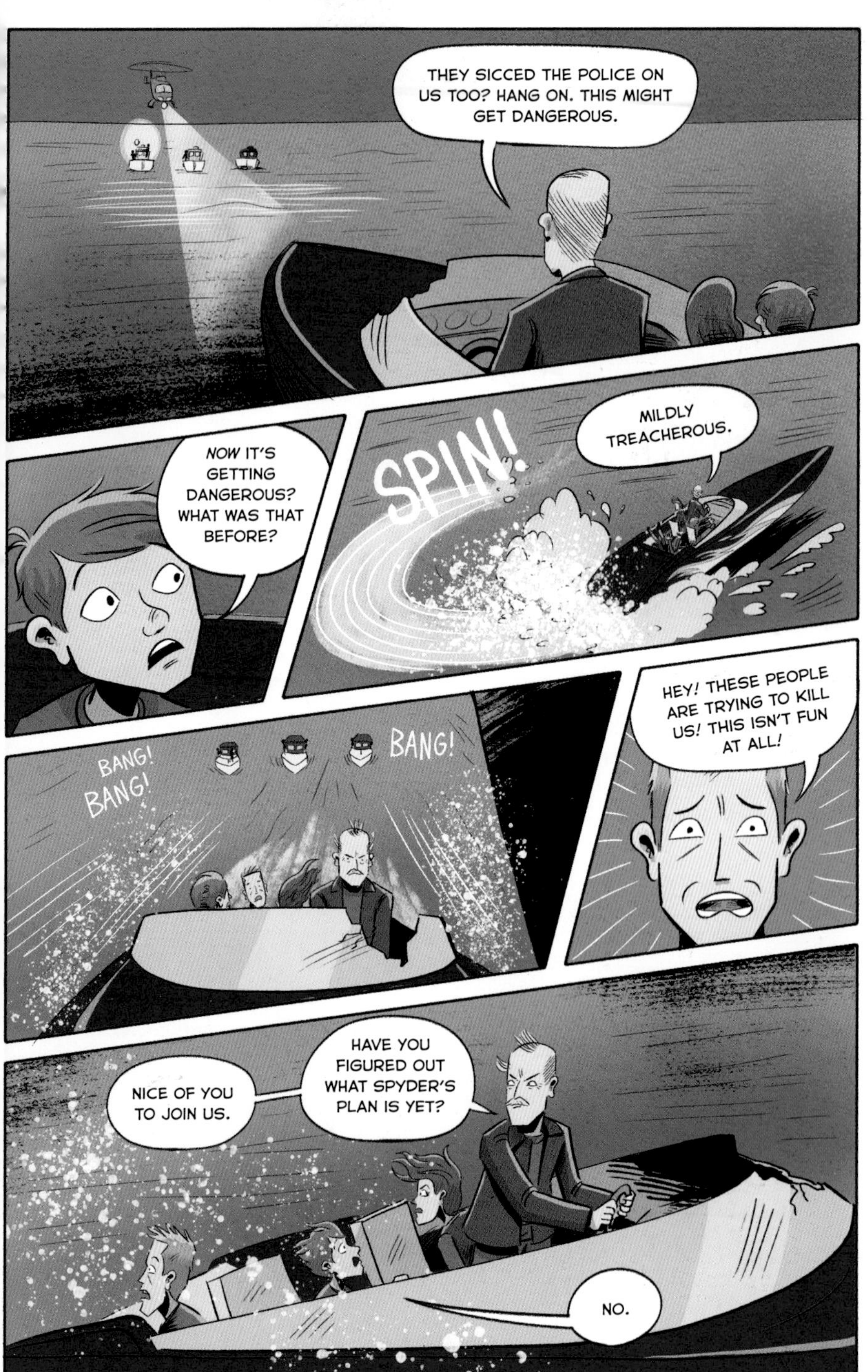
THEY SICCED THE POLICE ON US TOO? HANG ON. THIS MIGHT GET DANGEROUS.
*NOW* IT'S GETTING DANGEROUS? WHAT WAS THAT BEFORE?
SPIN!
MILDLY TREACHEROUS.
BANG! BANG!
BANG!
HEY! THESE PEOPLE ARE TRYING TO KILL US! THIS ISN'T FUN AT ALL!
NICE OF YOU TO JOIN US.
HAVE YOU FIGURED OUT WHAT SPYDER'S PLAN IS YET?
NO.

THEN THINK HARDER.
*THINK HARDER?* WHAT IS THAT EVEN SUPPOSED TO MEAN? THAT'S LIKE TELLING SOMEONE TO SEE HARDER OR TASTE HARDER. THE PROBLEM ISN'T THAT I'M NOT THINKING HARD ENOUGH. IT'S THAT YOUR PLAN TO SEND ME UNDERCOVER WASN'T ANY GOOD!
OUR PLAN WAS PERFECTLY FINE.
SWISH!
BANG!
WOOSH!
ARRGH!
AAAHH!
SPLASH!

SPYDER NEVER BELIEVED I WAS REALLY WORKING WITH THEM! THEY KNEW I WAS A MOLE THE WHOLE TIME. ANY INFORMATION THEY FED ME WAS FALSE!
THEY MIGHT HAVE *SUSPECTED* YOU WERE A MOLE, BUT THEY WEREN'T SURE. THEY WOULDN'T HAVE BROUGHT YOU IN MERELY TO SET US UP. THAT'D BE TOO RISKY. THEY *WANTED* YOU FOR SOMETHING.
BANG BANG!
NO THEY DIDN'T. I WAS JUST A PATSY.
YOU WERE NOT! SPYDER HAS ALWAYS WANTED YOU ON THEIR SIDE. BECAUSE YOU'RE NOT AS INCOMPETENT AS YOU THINK YOU ARE! SO *THINK!* WHAT DID THEY WANT YOU FOR?
I DON'T KNOW!
DID THEY ASK YOU TO DO ANYTHING UNUSUAL?
NO! I HAVEN'T DONE ANYTHING SINCE I GOT THERE EXCEPT TAKE CLASSES AND SOLVE MATH PROBLEMS!

OH.
WHAT IS IT?
I KNOW WHAT SPYDER'S UP TO...
SMASH!
WE'RE HIT! ABANDON SHIP!
WHAT?

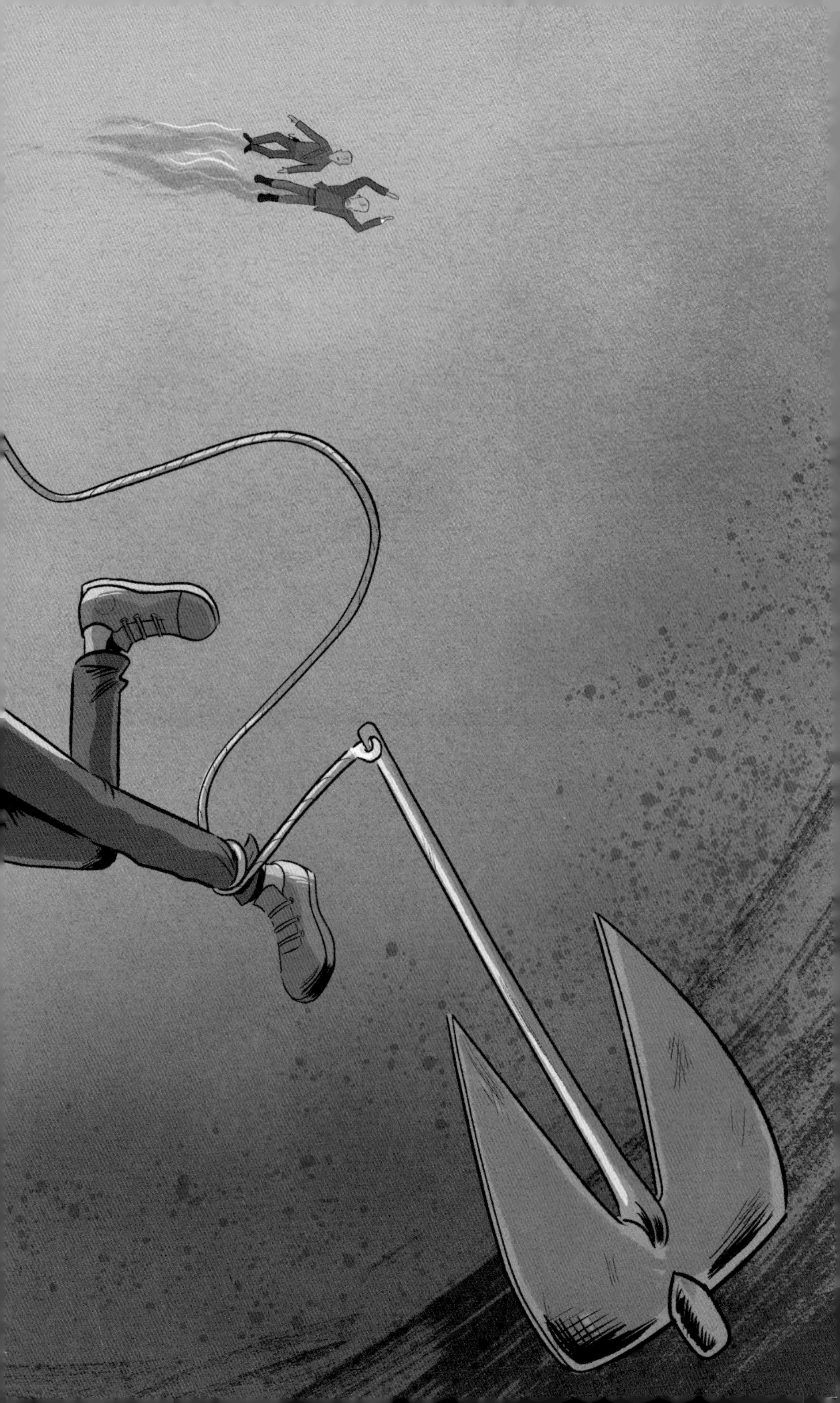

BOOM!

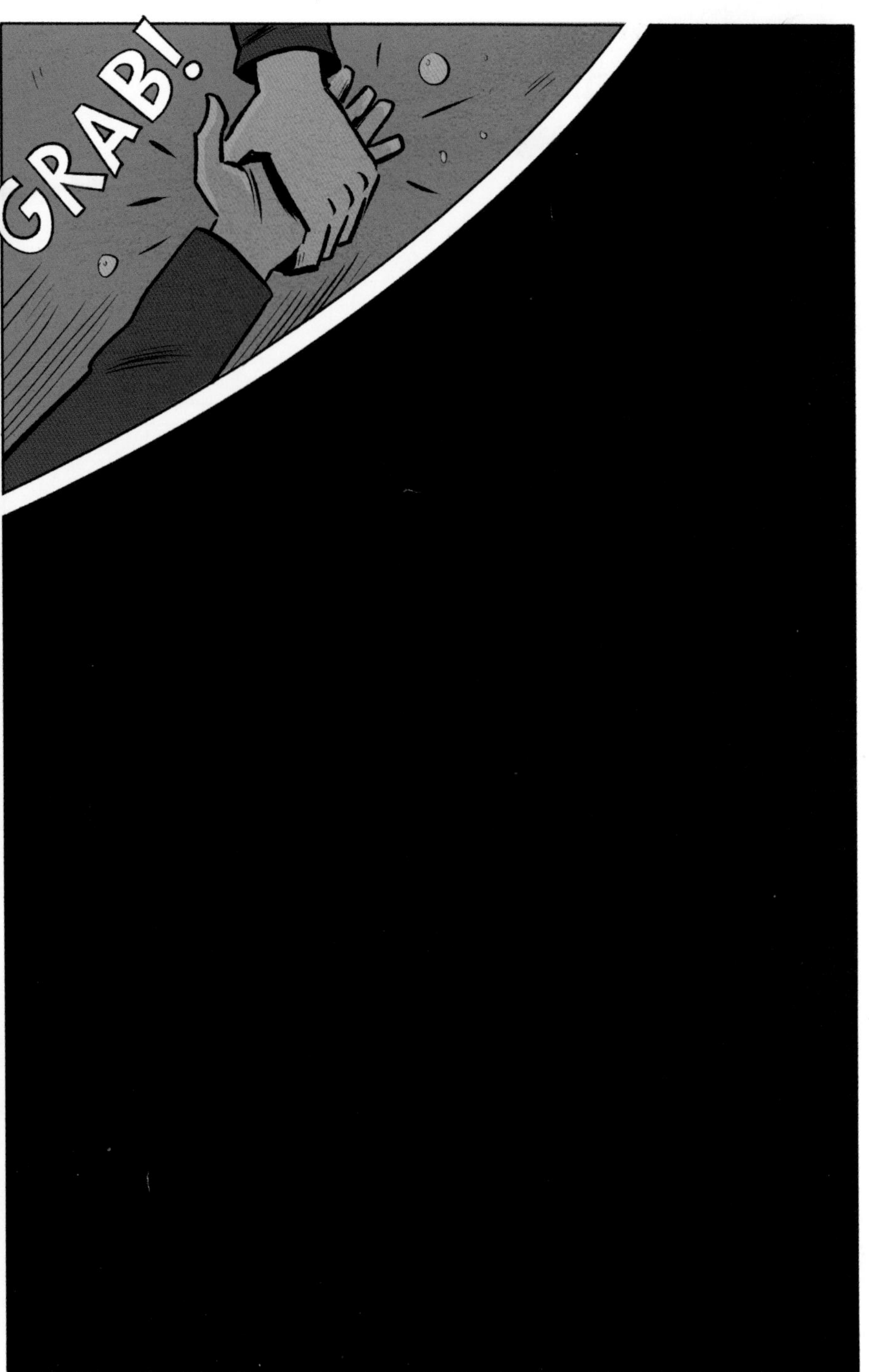
GRAB!

HE HASN'T REGAINED CONSCIOUSNESS YET, BUT HE'S STABLE...

HE NEEDS TIME TO RECOVER...

YES, I UNDERSTAND WHAT'S AT STAKE. WHAT'S THE SITUATION THERE?

LET ME GUESS. WE'RE INSIDE THE STATUE OF LIBERTY.

HE'S UP. I'LL CALL YOU BACK.

Souvenirs

WHAT HAPPENED?

OUR BOAT'S ANCHOR ROPE SNAGGED AROUND YOUR LEG. BY THE TIME I GOT YOU FREE, YOU WERE... WELL, IT COULD HAVE BEEN BAD.

YOU HAD TO RESUSCITATE ME?

YES.

DON'T GET ALL WORKED UP. YES, OUR LIPS TOUCHED. BUT IT WASN'T KISSING. I WAS ONLY FORCING AIR INTO YOUR LUNGS.

HOW'D WE GET IN HERE?

THERE'S A SECRET ENTRANCE. GRANDPA KNEW ABOUT IT.

DON'T TELL ME THE STATUE OF LIBERTY IS REALLY PART OF SOME TOP-SECRET NEW YORK CITY DEFENSE SYSTEM?

IT IS. BUT UNLIKE THE WASHINGTON MONUMENT, IT'S NOT THAT BIG A SECRET. THE MILITARY STARTED USING THIS ISLAND BACK IN 1807. THE FORT'S NOT EVEN HIDDEN. THEY PUT THE STATUE RIGHT ON TOP OF IT.

SOLDIERS WERE STATIONED HERE RIGHT UP THROUGH THE CIVIL WAR. THEN, IN THE 1870S, THE ARMY DECIDED IT NEEDED A LOOKOUT TOWER HERE TO DETECT THREATS COMING FROM THE SEA.

THIS STATUE WAS BUILT FOR SURVEILLANCE?
YOU DIDN'T REALLY THINK IT WAS A GIFT? FROM *FRANCE*? WHY WOULD FRANCE GIVE US A GIANT STATUE OF A WOMAN?

TO CELEBRATE OUR NATION'S HUNDREDTH BIRTHDAY.

OH, PLEASE. I CAN'T BELIEVE YOU BOUGHT THAT STORY.

I'M PRETTY SURE *EVERYONE* BOUGHT THAT STORY. EVEN THE PARK SERVICE.

ALL PART OF THE DISINFORMATION CAMPAIGN. HOW'S YOUR STRENGTH? CAN YOU CLIMB?
...YES?
THEN LET'S GO UP.

IT WAS ACTUALLY PRETTY BRILLIANT, MAKING THE SURVEILLANCE TOWER A STATUE. THE OBSERVATION PLATFORM IN THE CROWN IS HIGH ENOUGH TO SEE FOR THIRTY MILES IN ANY DIRECTION—AND, YET, THE ARMY ACTUALLY CONVINCED THE WHOLE WORLD THIS WAS JUST SOME BIZARRE ART PROJECT.
ARE ALEXANDER AND CYRUS IN THE CROWN RIGHT NOW?

YES. THEY'RE KEEPING AN EYE ON OUR SURROUNDINGS, WAITING FOR THE COAST TO BE CLEAR.
AREN'T THEY WORRIED THAT SOMEONE ELSE IN THE CIA KNOWS THE STATUE IS A FORTRESS AND WILL COME LOOKING FOR US HERE?
NO. APPARENTLY, MOST OF THE HISTORY OF THESE PLACES HAS BEEN FORGOTTEN, EVEN BY THE GOVERNMENT ITSELF.

AH, BEN! YOU'RE LOOKING WELL, ALL THINGS CONSIDERED.
GLAD TO SEE YOU'VE FINALLY DECIDED TO JOIN US.
HE WASN'T SLACKING OFF, GRANDPA. HE WAS UNCONSCIOUS.

YOU'D NEVER CATCH *ME* LOSING CONSCIOUSNESS IN THE MIDDLE OF A MISSION.
THE FEDS ARE STILL SEARCHING THE ISLAND.

SLAP!

RIGHT BEFORE THE BOAT BLEW, YOU SAID YOU KNEW WHAT SPYDER WAS PLANNING. CARE TO FINALLY SHARE THAT WITH US?

OH, RIGHT.
SPYDER'S GOING TO USE THOSE MISSILES TO DESTROY ALL THE BRIDGES AND TUNNELS CONNECTING MANHATTAN TO THE MAINLAND.
HOW DO YOU KNOW?

YOU WERE RIGHT. SPYDER *DID* WANT ME FOR SOMETHING. THE WHOLE TIME I'VE BEEN THERE, THEY'VE BEEN GIVING ME ALL THESE MATH PROBLEMS INVOLVING MISSILES. I THOUGHT THEY WERE FOR CLASS, BUT THEY WERE FOR A REAL ATTACK.
What angle of trajectory would the missile need to enter the water in order to destroy the tunnel 100 feet below?

WHAT KIND OF PROBLEMS WERE THEY?

COMPLEX TARGETING ISSUES, MOSTLY. LIKE, *REALLY* COMPLEX. I GAVE SPYDER EVERYTHING THEY'D NEED TO PROGRAM THEIR MISSILES TO HIT PRECISE TARGETS AROUND HERE.

AND THEY RECRUITED A *KID* TO DO THAT?
BEN ISN'T A NORMAL KID. WHEN IT COMES TO MATH, THERE'S NOT MANY *ADULTS* WHO CAN DO WHAT HE CAN. WE PRACTICALLY GIFT-WRAPPED HIM FOR SPYDER.

PLUS, I HAD THE ADDED BONUS OF SECRETLY WORKING FOR YOU. NOT ONLY DID SPYDER GET ME TO DO THEIR DIRTY WORK FOR THEM, BUT THEY ALSO USED ME TO FEED YOU FALSE INFORMATION.

THEY'RE ALWAYS ONE STEP AHEAD OF US. IF NOT TWENTY.

BUT NOW WE KNOW WHAT THEIR PLAN IS. THAT'S SOMETHING, RIGHT?

WE *THINK* WE KNOW WHAT THEIR PLAN IS. I HAVEN'T HEARD MUCH EVIDENCE TO SUPPORT THIS IDEA YET.

WHAT ELSE DO YOU HAVE?

I'M PRETTY SURE JOSHUA HALLAL PROGRAMMED THE MISSILES. THAT'S WHAT HE WAS DOING IN THE UNDERGROUND LAIR THE NIGHT I SAW HIM, WHEN HE WAS USING RUSSIAN. SPYDER GOT RUSSIAN MISSILES BEFORE. THEY COULD DO IT AGAIN.

TAP TAP TAP!

BUT YOU DON'T SPEAK RUSSIAN. SO YOU CAN'T BE SURE.
TRUE. BUT I DO REMEMBER NUMBERS WELL. JOSHUA ENTERED 40.7057 AND 73.9964. IF HE WAS PROGRAMMING MISSILES, THEN THOSE ARE PROBABLY COORDINATES.
TAP TAP!

THOSE ARE COORDINATES, ALL RIGHT...FOR THE BROOKLYN BRIDGE.

THEY ALSO HAD ME DO PROBLEMS ABOUT HOW MUCH EXPLOSIVE WAS NEEDED TO BLOW UP BRIDGES AND TUNNELS.

I WORKED OUT THE PAYLOADS AND THE BEST PLACES TO STRIKE THE TARGETS TO PROVIDE MAXIMUM DAMAGE...

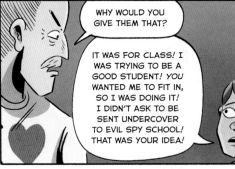

WHY WOULD YOU GIVE THEM THAT?

IT WAS FOR CLASS! I WAS TRYING TO BE A GOOD STUDENT! *YOU* WANTED ME TO FIT IN, SO I WAS DOING IT! I DIDN'T ASK TO BE SENT UNDERCOVER TO EVIL SPY SCHOOL! THAT WAS YOUR IDEA!

BEN'S RIGHT, GRANDPA. ABOUT EVERYTHING, I THINK. THAT DAY AT SANDY HOOK, MURRAY WASN'T ONLY TAKING PICTURES OF THE MISSILE SILOS.
HE WAS ALSO PHOTOGRAPHING THE BRIDGES OF NEW YORK CITY. SPYDER JUST DESTROYED THE MISSILES DESIGNED TO PROTECT NEW YORK. SO NOW THERE'S NOTHING TO STOP THEM FROM ATTACKING. EXCEPT US.

CLICK! CLICK! CLICK!

HOW ARE WE SUPPOSED TO DO THAT? WE HAVE NO IDEA WHERE SPYDER'S MISSILES ARE.
THAT'S NOT POSSIBLE. WE'VE BEEN WATCHING THAT PLACE FOR WEEKS.
YES WE DO. THEY'RE BACK AT HIDDEN FOREST.
I ♥ NY

THE MISSILES MUST HAVE BEEN THERE THE WHOLE TIME.

YOU'RE TELLING US THAT SPYDER HID A BUNCH OF STOLEN MISSILES IN A SUBURBAN HOUSING DEVELOPMENT?

IT'S NOT A REAL HOUSING DEVELOPMENT. IT'S CAMOUFLAGE FOR THE MISSILES. SPYDER'S HIDING THEM IN PLAIN SIGHT.

BUT THERE'S NO SILOS.
YES THERE *ARE*. THEY'RE DISGUISED AS SEPTIC TANKS.
I ♥ NY

THE OTHER NIGHT, I WAS ON TOP OF ONE, AND THERE WAS A BIG HINGE ON THE EDGE OF IT.

THE ONLY REASON YOU'D HAVE A HINGE THERE IS IF THE TOP WAS SUPPOSED TO SWING OPEN, AND YOU DON'T NEED THE TOP TO SWING OPEN ON A SEPTIC TANK...

BUT YOU *DO* ON A MISSILE SILO. GOOD GRAVY, THAT PLACE ISN'T FAR FROM NEW YORK AT ALL!

THAT'S ONLY THE SHADOW FORCE. LOOKS LIKE MOST EVERYONE ELSE HAS BEEN SENT HOME. BESIDES, WE NEED AT LEAST ONE TEAM HERE SO WE CAN GET OFF THIS ISLAND.

HOW SO?

BECAUSE WE'RE GONNA STEAL THEIR BOAT.

AND THEN WHAT? THE FOUR OF US CAN'T INFILTRATE HIDDEN FOREST BY OURSELVES. THE SECURITY IS EXTREME—AND THE CONTROL CENTER IS IN THE MIDDLE OF THE COMPLEX, TWO STORIES UNDERGROUND.

WE'D NEED A WHOLE PLATOON OF AGENTS TO EVEN MAKE A DENT IN THAT PLACE. IS THERE *ANY* CIA AGENT WE CAN TRUST? ANYONE WE CAN EXPLAIN THE SITUATION TO?

NOT THAT I CAN THINK OF.
I KNOW HOW TO GET THE CIA TO HIDDEN FOREST. WE JUST NEED THE RIGHT BAIT.

AND WHAT WOULD THAT BE?

US.

STORAGE

SECURITY
SECURITY

CREAK!

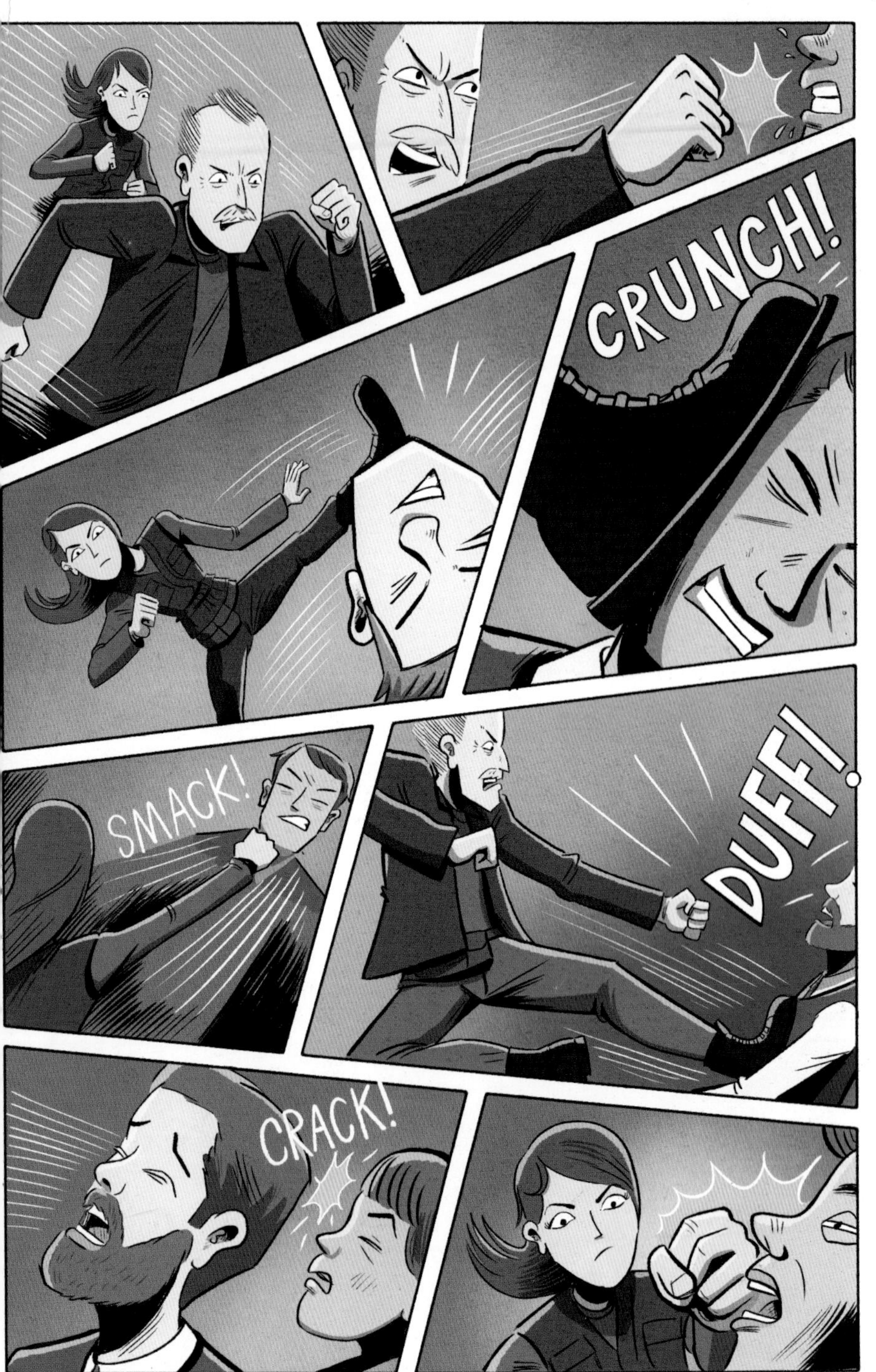
CRUNCH!
SMACK!
DUFF!
CRACK!

THIS PLAN OF YOURS BETTER WORK.

TAP!
TAP!
HELLO?
HEY. IT'S BEN.

SMOKESCREEN?! WHAT'S HAPPENING? WORD IS THAT YOU AND THE HALES HAVE JOINED THE DARK SIDE. I DON'T BELIEVE IT, OF COURSE, BUT THE REST OF THE CIA SEEMS TO.

BELIEVE IT. I *HAVE* JOINED THE DARK SIDE.


NO, YOU HAVEN'T. IF YOU'D REALLY JOINED THE DARK SIDE, YOU WOULDN'T BE TELLING ME THAT YOU HAD. YOU'D BE TELLING ME THAT YOU HADN'T.

SO IF I SAID I HADN'T JOINED THE DARK SIDE, THEN YOU'D THINK I HAD?


NEVER. I KNOW YOU, BEN. I KNOW YOU'RE NOT A TRAITOR.

I AM, ZOE. I SWEAR. I'M A TRAITOR TO MY COUNTRY AND VERY, VERY DANGEROUS. SO I NEED YOU TO ALERT THE SCHOOL ADMINISTRATION THAT YOU KNOW EXACTLY WHERE I'M GOING TO BE TWO HOURS FROM NOW.

I'M NOT GOING TO DO THAT. YOU'RE MY FRIEND. WHY WOULD I TURN YOU IN?

BECAUSE I'M WORKING WITH SPYDER NOW, AND WE'RE ABOUT TO LAUNCH MISSILES AT NEW YORK CITY.
WHAT?!
GET A PEN. I'M GOING TO GIVE YOU THE EXACT COORDINATES OF WHERE I'M GOING TO BE.

SWIPE!
OKAY.

40.7407° NORTH, 74.3639° WEST. I NEED YOU TO REPORT THIS TO THE ADMINISTRATION RIGHT AWAY. TELL THEM THAT YOU FIGURED OUT WHERE I'VE BEEN. TELL THEM YOU ALWAYS SUSPECTED I WAS NO GOOD, AND SO YOU PUT A TRACER ON ME.

THEY'LL NEVER BELIEVE THAT I WAS SUSPICIOUS OF YOU. I'M ALWAYS GOING ON ABOUT HOW GREAT YOU ARE.

WHICH YOU ONLY DID SO THAT I'D DROP MY GUARD AROUND YOU AND LET YOU GET CLOSE TO ME. VERY SNEAKY OF YOU, REALLY. PROBABLY WORTH SOME SORT OF COMMENDATION WHEN THE CIA FOLLOWS UP ON YOUR TIP AND CAPTURES ME.

BEN, THIS IS CRAZY.
HONESTLY, IT'S NOT EVEN IN THE TOP THREE CRAZIEST THINGS I'VE DONE TODAY.

CAN YOU AT LEAST EXPLAIN WHAT'S GOING ON?

IT'D TAKE WAY TOO LONG. I NEED YOU TO DO THIS *RIGHT NOW*. EVERY SECOND COUNTS.

ALL RIGHT. I'LL TURN YOU IN.

THANKS. YOU'RE A GOOD FRIEND.

LEW BROTHERS
CONSTRUCTION
LEW BROTHERS.
OH MY GOSH...

LOOKS LIKE THE CIA BEAT US HERE.

BUT THE AGENTS ARE SO FOCUSED ON HIDDEN FOREST THAT THEY HAVEN'T SEEN US.

MAYBE BEN AND I OUGHT TO STAY BEHIND...IN CASE YOU NEED BACKUP LATER ON.
FRANKLY, I'D PREFER A GREENHORN LIKE BEN STAY WELL CLEAR OF THE ACTION.
BUT YOU'RE THE ONLY ONE WHO'S BEEN INSIDE SPYDER'S LAIR. THAT MAKES YOU A KEY ASSET.

SPYDER! WE KNOW YOU'RE IN THERE! THIS IS THE CENTRAL INTELLIGENCE AGENCY. WE HAVE YOU SURROUNDED. CEASE ALL HOSTILE ACTS AT ONCE OR WE WILL HAVE NO CHOICE BUT TO TAKE YOU BY FORCE!

DO YOU BELIEVE THIS GUY? TIME IS OF THE ESSENCE AND HE'S GIVING WARNINGS LIKE A HALL MONITOR. WE NEED TO KICK THIS ASSAULT IN GEAR.

BANG!
BANG!

CRACK!
BLAM!

LOB!
POW!
BOOM!
POW!

POW!
BOOM!
BANG!

WHIZZ!

CLIP!
CLIP!

BANG!
BANG!
WAAWAAWAAWA

BANG!
BANG!

GET GOING! WE'LL DRAW THEIR FIRE!
WE WILL?!
BANG!
BOOM!
BANG!
BANG!

RRRRRRRRRR
RRRRRRRRRRR
THEY'RE PREPARING TO FIRE! WE DON'T HAVE MUCH TIME!

BANG!
BANG!
WHIZZ!

TWIST!
YOU CAN STOP POKING AROUND OUT THERE! THE PARTY'S IN HERE!

YOU DIDN'T REALLY THINK YOU COULD SNEAK UP ON US IN HERE, DID YOU? WE KNEW YOU'D BE COMING. THIS IS YOUR STANDARD MOVE.
SPYDER'S ABOUT TO PUT A PLAN INTO ACTION; YOU ARRIVE JUST MINUTES BEFORE IT HAPPENS AND TRY TO THWART IT. LIKE CLOCKWORK.

OH, WE'RE NOT *TRYING* TO THWART YOUR PLANS. WE'RE THWARTING THEM. SHUT OFF THE MISSILES.

IT CAN'T BE DONE. EVERYTHING IS PREPROGRAMMED.

I WASN'T TALKING TO YOU. I KNOW YOU'RE NOT SMART ENOUGH TO CONTROL THE MISSILES.
RIP!

NEFARIOUS, ABORT THE MISSILES OR YOU'LL BOTH BE SORRY.

HOW ABOUT THIS INSTEAD? YOU DROP YOUR WEAPONS, OR ASHLEY SHISH KEBABS BOTH OF YOU.

HELLO,
JIDIOTS.

I REALLY DON'T WANT TO HURT YOU, BUT I WILL. DROP THE WEAPON.

SORRY, BUT THERE'LL BE NO THWARTING OUR PLANS TONIGHT.
DROP!

BLE!
RUMBLE!
RUMB

ROAR

ROAR!

HOW LONG WILL IT TAKE THOSE TO HIT THEIR TARGETS?
THE FIRST WILL STRIKE IN EIGHT MINUTES.

YOU HAVE TO ABORT THOSE MISSILES. IF YOU DON'T, YOU'RE GOING TO HAVE THE BLOOD OF THOUSANDS OF INNOCENT PEOPLE ON YOUR HANDS.
THIS ISN'T ABOUT KILLING PEOPLE. YOU DON'T HAVE ANY IDEA WHAT WE'RE REALLY DOING HERE.

YES I DO. YOU'RE NOT BLOWING UP ALL THE MAJOR BRIDGES AROUND MANHATTAN JUST TO CAUSE CHAOS. YOU'RE DOING IT SO THAT YOU CAN GET PAID BILLIONS TO REBUILD THEM.

HOLY COW! YOU FIGURED OUT OUR EVIL SCHEME *AGAIN!* EVERY TIME I THINK WE'VE GOT YOU FOOLED, YOU STILL WORK IT OUT. HOW'D YOU DO IT THIS TIME, BRAINIAC?

I SAW A LEW BROTHERS CONSTRUCTION SITE IN NEW JERSEY. A BIG ONE, REBUILDING AN ENTIRE SHIPPING PIER. WHICH MEANT SPYDER'S CONSTRUCTION COMPANY WAS MUCH BIGGER THAN I REALIZED. SO WE GOOGLED THE COMPANY. WITH THE EXCEPTION OF THIS COMMUNITY, LEW BROTHERS ONLY DOES GOVERNMENT WORK. MOSTLY LARGE INFRASTRUCTURE PROJECTS. LIKE BRIDGES. AND TUNNELS.

NICE WORK, AS USUAL.
WE ORIGINALLY STARTED LEW BROTHERS AS A MONEY-LAUNDERING SCHEME, BUT THEN FOUND THAT BEING EVIL IS STANDARD PROCEDURE IN THE LARGE-SCALE CONSTRUCTION BUSINESS. IN FACT, WE WERE SHOCKED BY HOW CORRUPT SOME OF OUR RIVAL COMPANIES WERE—AND WE'RE TERRORISTS!

SWING!

BEFORE WE KNEW IT, LEW BROTHERS WAS BRINGING IN MORE MONEY THAN OUR ILLEGAL SCHEMES. SO THEN WE STARTED THINKING: WHY WAIT FOR THE GOVERNMENT TO COME TO *US* WITH CONSTRUCTION JOBS? WHY NOT CREATE THE JOBS OURSELVES? THE REAL MONEY ISN'T IN KNOCKING THINGS DOWN; IT'S IN PUTTING THEM BACK UP AGAIN.
ROAR!

SO WHY SHOULD WE LET SOME OTHER SLEAZEBALLS MAKE BIG PROFITS FROM OUR TERRORISM WHEN *WE* COULD BE THE SLEAZEBALLS MAKING BIG PROFITS OURSELVES?
LEW BROTHERS CONSTRUCTION
DUFF!

YOU'RE CREATING A FAKE TERRORIST ATTACK JUST TO CASH IN ON THE EMERGENCY REBUILDING FUNDS?

YES!

SO, YOU SEE, WHAT WE'RE DOING HERE ISN'T SO BAD, REALLY. IT'S NOT SLAUGHTER-THOUSANDS-OF-INNOCENT-PEOPLE EVIL. IT'S MORE LIKE INCONVENIENCE-MILLIONS-OF-PEOPLE-FOR-A-FEW-YEARS EVIL.

PEOPLE ARE STILL GOING TO BE HURT! AND WHAT DO YOU THINK WILL HAPPEN TO EVERYONE IN MANHATTAN AFTER YOU CUT THEM OFF FROM THE REST OF THE COUNTRY? THERE'LL BE PANICS. FOOD SHORTAGES. RIOTS! WHAT YOU'RE DOING HERE IS GOING TO LEAD TO GREAT SUFFERING, JUST SO YOU CAN MAKE SOME MONEY.
WE'RE NOT HAPPY.
BOO!

YOU'VE GOT IT WRONG.
NO, I DON'T.
YOU DO. WE'RE NOT GOING TO JUST MAKE *SOME* MONEY. WE'RE GOING TO MAKE *AN INCREDIBLE AMOUNT* OF MONEY.

YOU THINK THOSE PEOPLE ARE GOING TO SUFFER? WELL, NO ONE HAS SUFFERED LIKE ME! I TRAINED MY WHOLE LIFE FOR THE OLYMPICS! I GAVE UP MY ENTIRE CHILDHOOD TO PRACTICE SIXTEEN HOURS A DAY!

I NEVER HAD FUN! I NEVER HAD FRIENDS! I NEVER HAD A SINGLE PIECE OF CANDY! AND FOR WHAT? SO SOME AWFUL JUDGE COULD MAKE A MISTAKE ON MY SCORE AND KEEP ME FROM MY RIGHTFUL PLACE ON TEAM USA!

I SAW THE OLYMPIC TRIALS. YOU DIDN'T DESERVE TO MAKE THE TEAM. YOU BLEW THAT LANDING.

I DID NOT! I STUCK THAT LANDING!

I STUCK IT!!!

SLAP!
BLOCK!

SWISH!

SWOOSH!
CHEEZ-Os

PULL!
AUTO-PILOT
DISENGAGED
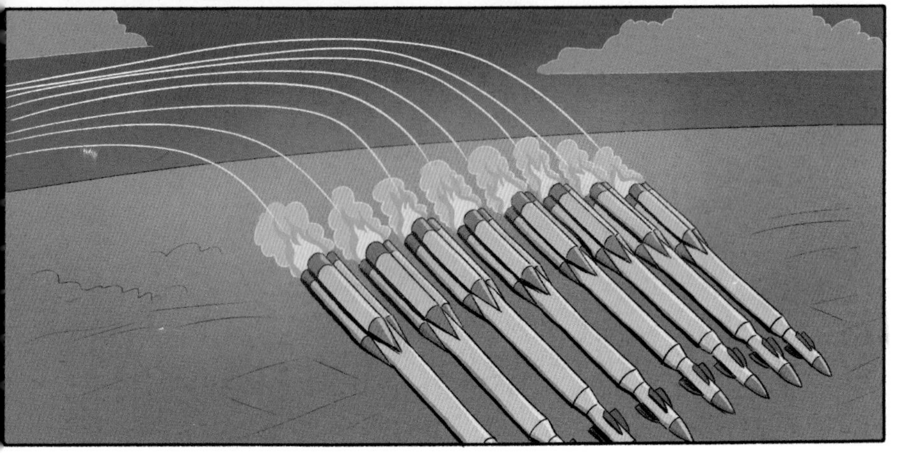

THE NAVIGATION SYSTEMS ARE BLOWN.
GUESS IT'S UP TO YOU, THEN.
WOOSH!

CLICK!

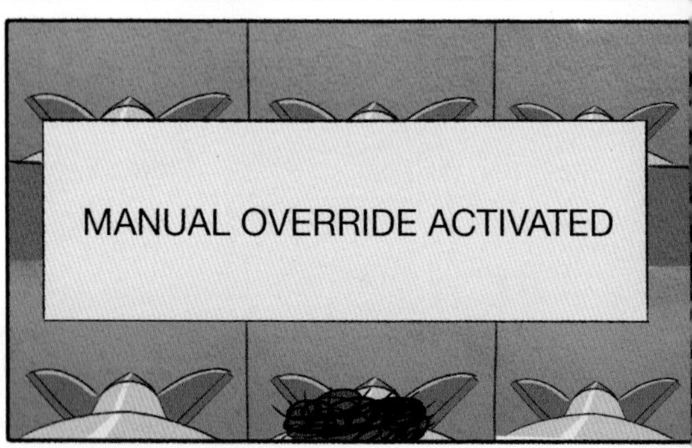
MANUAL OVERRIDE ACTIVATED

ROAR!

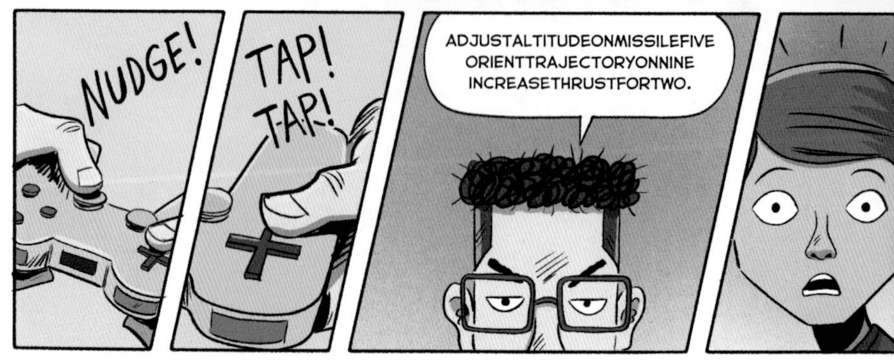
NUDGE!
TAP! TAP!
ADJUSTALTITUDEONMISSILEFIVE ORIENTTRAJECTORYONNINE INCREASETHRUSTFORTWO.

YOU WEREN'T JUST PLAYING GAMES. YOU WERE *PRACTICING*.
SWOOSH!

OH NO. IT'S NOT GOING TO BE THAT EASY, BEN.
ADAPTTOWIND SHEARFORMISSILE THREE...

JUST STAB HIM! KILL BEN BEFORE HE THWARTS US AGAIN!
DODGE!

HE'S NOT GOING TO THWART US THIS TIME. IT'S OUT OF HIS HANDS.

SO WHAT? DO IT ANYHOW! HE'S THE ENEMY!
BLOCK!

YOU ACTUALLY HAD A CRUSH ON THIS GIRL? SHE'S NUTS.
DODGE!
APPARENTLY, I MISJUDGED HER.
GEE, YOU THINK?

NEFARIOUS, THINK ABOUT WHAT YOU'RE DOING. THIS ISN'T A GAME ANYMORE. WHEN THOSE MISSILES STRIKE, IT WILL HAPPEN IN THE REAL WORLD.
AND YOU'LL MAKE *REAL* MONEY! TONS OF IT!

NO, YOU WON'T. SPYDER ONLY TOLD YOU GUYS THAT TO GET YOU TO DO THEIR DIRTY WORK FOR THEM.

DON'T LISTEN TO HIM! NO ONE AT SPYDER CONNED US! THEY WOULDN'T DO THAT TO ME!

THEN WHERE ARE THEY? I HAVEN'T SEEN THEM ANYWHERE AROUND HERE TONIGHT. JOSHUA TOLD US HIMSELF THAT SPYDER WAS GOING TO GET AWAY WITH THIS BECAUSE ALL THE EVIDENCE WOULD POINT TO SOME FALL GUYS. WELL, *YOU'RE* THE FALL GUYS.
SWISH!

FLIP!

NO. SPYDER'S FRAMING TERRORISTS FOR THIS.

SPYDER'S FRAMING *YOU*. JOSHUA AND THE TOP BRASS WILL MAKE BILLIONS—AND YOU'LL END UP IN JAIL.
NEFARIOUS, HE'S LYING TO YOU! STAY ON COURSE!

WHOOSH!

THE PEOPLE AT SPYDER AREN'T YOUR FRIENDS. THEY'RE USING YOU. IF YOU WANT TO MAKE *REAL* FRIENDS, YOU DON'T DO IT BY BEING THE BAD GUY. YOU DO IT BY BEING THE HERO. AND THIS IS YOUR CHANCE. YOU CAN SAVE THE CITY!

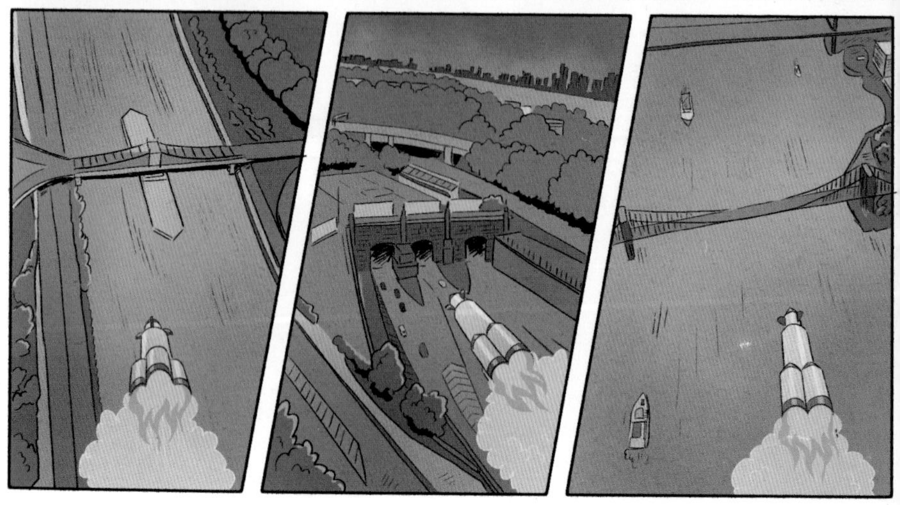

ROAR!
ROAR!
WHOOSH!

DODGE!
SWISH!
CLICK!
TAP! TAP!
TAP!
TWIST!
NUDGE!
CLICK!
WOOSH!
VROOM!
ROAR!
FWSSH!

NOOOO! YOU FOOL! WHAT ARE YOU DOING?! BRING THEM BACK AROUND!

TAP!
TAP!
TAP!

SO WE'LL GET CAUGHT! SPYDER WILL FIND A WAY TO SPRING US!
BLOCK!
ROAR!
ROAR!
WHY WOULD THEY? THEN THEY'D JUST HAVE TO SHARE THE MONEY WITH US. AND THEY'RE NOT GOING TO DO THAT. AFTER ALL, THEY'RE EVIL.
SWISH!
YOU CAN STILL FIX THIS! EVEN IF YOU ONLY HIT A FEW OF THE TARGETS, WE'LL STILL BE RICH! DON'T LET BEN CONFUSE YOU! SPYDER ISN'T THE ENEMY HERE! *HE* IS! HE'S–

OOF!
CRACK!
BOOM!

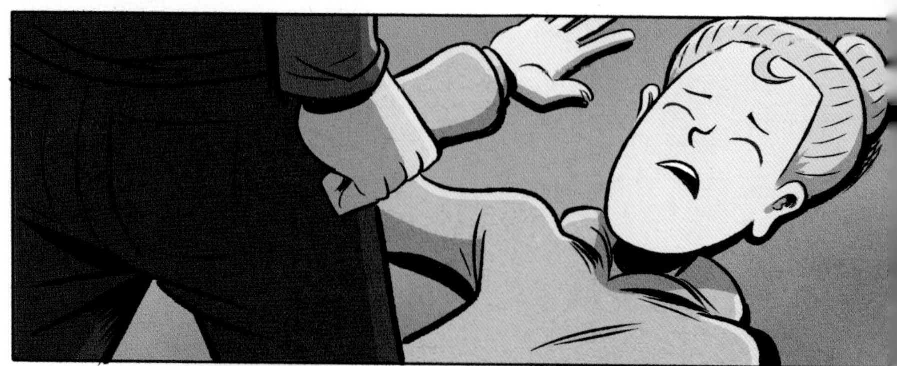

WHAT'S HAPPENING THERE? WHAT ARE YOU DOING WITH THAT LAST MISSILE?

I'M NOT DOING *ANYTHING* WITH IT. I DON'T HAVE CONTROL OVER IT ANYMORE.
TAP TAP TAP!

THEN WHERE'S IT GOING?
HERE.
I DID THE MATH FOR THIS, TOO. IT WAS FOR EXTRA CREDIT. THERE'S A FAIL-SAFE BUILT INTO THAT ROCKET IN CASE THINGS GO WRONG. A HOMING DEVICE.

WHY WOULD THEY SEND A MISSILE *HERE* IF THINGS GO WRONG?

NO LOOSE ENDS. YOU ALL KNOW TOO MUCH. BUT THE CIA CAN'T MAKE YOU TALK IF YOU'RE DEAD.
YOU MEAN THEY'RE GOING TO KILL ME?! *ME?* I'M MURRAY! THEY LOVE ME HERE! THEY TOLD ME I WAS IMPORTANT! THEY TOLD ME I'D GET RICH!
THEY LIED TO YOU. YOU'RE EXPENDABLE.

HOW MUCH TIME DO WE HAVE?

EIGHT MINUTES.

LET'S GET OUT OF HERE!

NOT SO FAST.

YOU JIDIOTS AREN'T GOING ANYWHERE!
JIDIOTS?
JERKS PLUS IDIOTS.
THAT'S RIGHT! WE'RE STAYING RIGHT HERE UNTIL...
WHACK!

HEY, BEN!

ZOE? WHAT ARE YOU DOING HERE?

I'M ON A FIELD TRIP! THE CIA LET ME COME ON THE MISSION AS A REWARD FOR TURNING YOU IN! I FLEW UP HERE ON A HELICOPTER WITH SOME BIG-SHOT AGENTS FROM WASHINGTON. IT WAS SUPER COOL!

I TOLD YOU FRIENDS COULD BE ASSETS.

WE HAVE TO EVACUATE. A MISSILE'S EN ROUTE TO BLOW US UP.
WHAT?! WHY?!
IT'S A LONG STORY.

THEY HAVE A SUNDAE MACHINE?!

HOW'D YOU FIND ME DOWN HERE?
OH, IT WAS JAWA'S IDEA TO SEARCH THIS BUILDING.
JAWA'S HERE TOO?
SPY SCHOOL LET ME PICK THREE FRIENDS TO COME ALONG. SO I BROUGHT JAWA, 'CAUSE HE'S ALMOST AS SMART AS YOU; CHIP, 'CAUSE HE'S TOUGH; AND WARREN, BECAUSE HE'D HAVE THROWN A FIT IF I DIDN'T PICK HIM.
ROAR!

IT'S QUIET. DID THE CIA WIN?
BIG-TIME. IT WAS PRETTY MUCH OVER BY THE TIME WE GOT HERE. ALL SPYDER'S GUYS WERE SURRENDERING. ALTHOUGH MOST CLAIMED THEY DIDN'T EVEN KNOW WHAT SPYDER WAS. THEY SAID THEY WERE ALL INDEPENDENT CONTRACTORS.
WHERE'S EVERYONE NOW?
THEY EVACUATED.

WE SHOULD EVACUATE TOO! IT SEEMS LIKE SOMETHING BAD IS GOING TO HAPPEN TO THIS PLACE.
THEN WHY ARE YOU STILL HERE?
WE WERE LOOKING FOR *YOU*.
AW, YOU GUYS ARE SO SWEET!
IT WAS MY IDEA.
WE'VE ONLY GOT FOUR MINUTES UNTIL DETONATION.

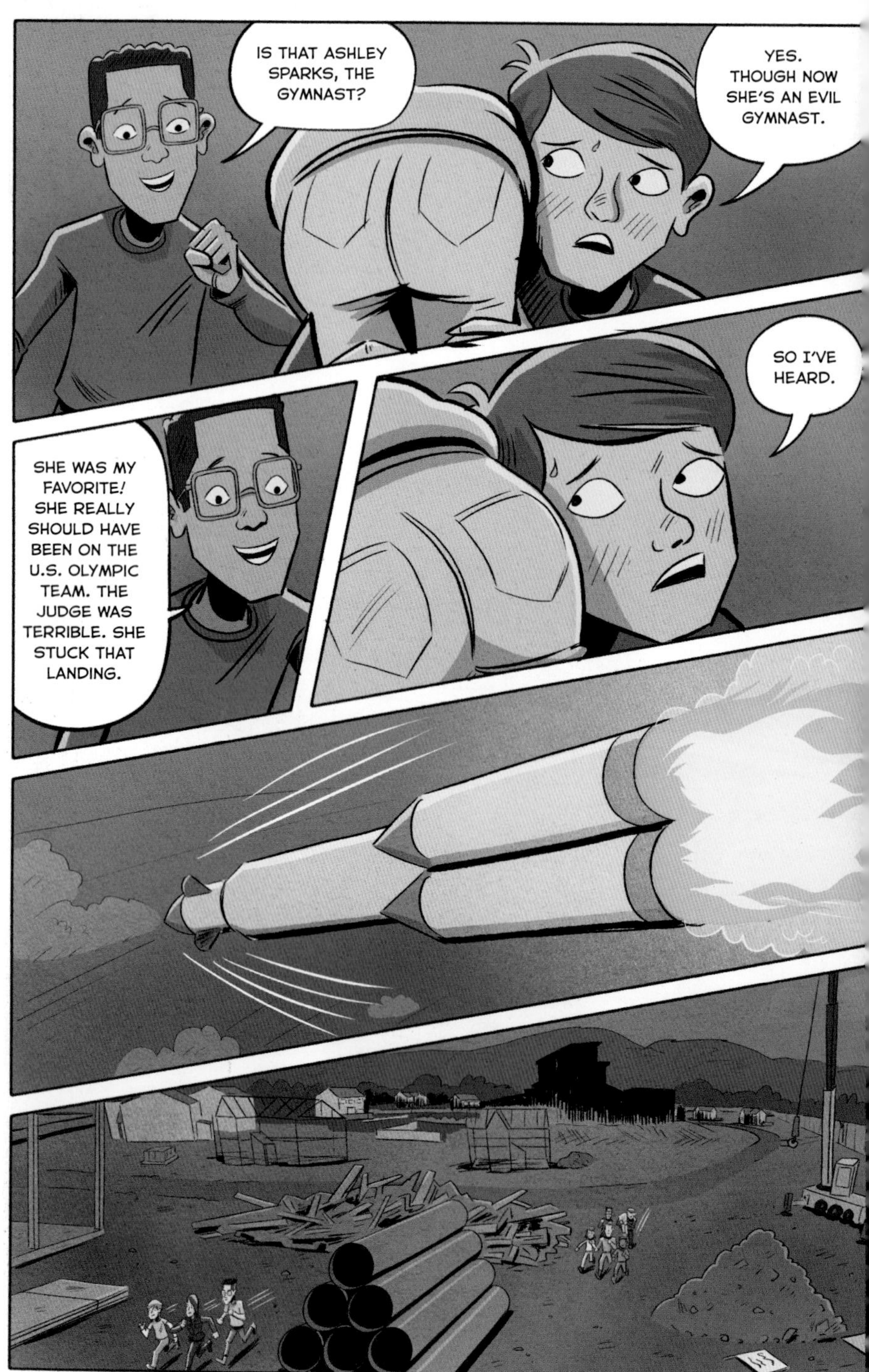
IS THAT ASHLEY SPARKS, THE GYMNAST?
YES. THOUGH NOW SHE'S AN EVIL GYMNAST.
SHE WAS MY FAVORITE! SHE REALLY SHOULD HAVE BEEN ON THE U.S. OLYMPIC TEAM. THE JUDGE WAS TERRIBLE. SHE STUCK THAT LANDING.
SO I'VE HEARD.

SHOVE!
THAT WAS ERICA.
AHHH!
TAKE HER TO THE AUTHORITIES. CATCH MURRAY AND THE OTHER GUY. I'LL FIND ERICA.

ERICA!
WHERE ARE YOU?
NEVER MIND ME! THERE'S NO TIME! SAVE YOURSELF!
JUST TELL ME WHERE YOU ARE!
NO!

GO AWAY! IF YOU TRY TO HELP ME, WE'LL BOTH DIE!
I'M NOT LEAVING YOU! YOU'RE MY FRIEND.
I TOLD YOU, HAVING FRIENDS IN THIS BUSINESS ONLY CAUSES TROUBLE.
FWOOSH!

GRAB THIS!
NO. I'LL PULL YOU IN.
JUST GRAB IT!

YOU'RE TOO NICE FOR YOUR OWN GOOD.

ROAR!

TAKE COVER!

KA

BOOM!

GAS LEAK DESTROYS GATED COMMUNITY.
NICE WORK, CYRUS... AND ALEXANDER.

I STUCK THE LANDING! I STUCK THE LANDING!
YOU REALLY PREVENTED ALL THOSE MISSILES FROM BLOWING UP THE CITY?
YEAH.
THAT'S AWESOME!
IT'S A SHAME THAT MURRAY GOT AWAY THOUGH.
WE'LL GET HIM SOMEDAY.

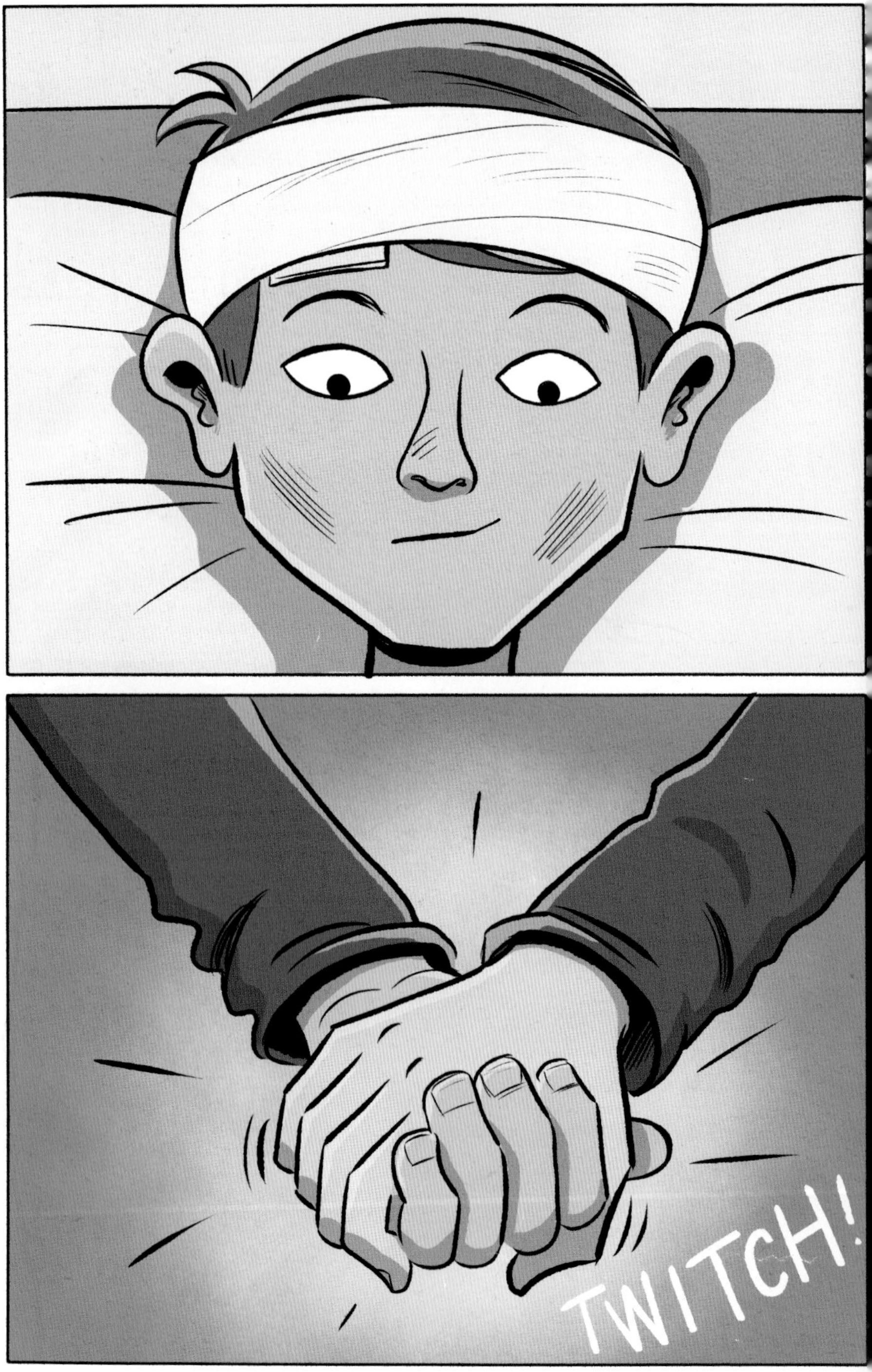

TWITCH!

HEY.
HEY. HOW ARE YOU FEELING?

EXCELLENT. BUT THAT'S PROBABLY BECAUSE THEY'VE GIVEN US PAINKILLERS. THANKS FOR SAVING ME. I OWE YOU ONE.

HOW ABOUT THIS: NEXT TIME YOU DECIDE TO BRING ME ON A MISSION, YOU TELL ME ABOUT IT FIRST?

DEAL. IN FACT, NEXT MISSION, I'LL ASK THEM TO MAKE US EQUAL PARTNERS.
REALLY? YOU'D DO THAT FOR ME?

OF COURSE. THAT'S WHAT FRIENDS ARE FOR.

DINER
CLOSED

September 20

To: CIA Director

Re: Operation Bedbug Mission Recap

While Operation Bedbug achieved its main objective—the discovery and subsequent thwarting of SPYDER's plans—I hesitate to call it a success.

The identities of the top members of said organization remain a mystery, while and managed to escape. The people we did capture were mere pawns of the organization, though Nefarious Jones has been eager to share what he knows. Given his aid in deflecting the missiles, he might have some value as

Sadly, Mr. Jones is unaware of what SPYDER's future plans might be and any further evidence concerning those was destroyed in Thus, it will require to determine what they are plotting next, although we can assume the organization suffered a severe financial loss from the failure of this endeavor.

Although Agent-to-Be Ripley he certainly proved his mettle on this mission—and I'm not saying that simply because he saved my granddaughter's life. Given their key contributions to Operation Bedbug and I suggest that both Erica and Benjamin should be reinstated as students at the Academy of Espionage—and given top grades in Undercover Work as well.

In addition, I would highly recommend the services of Ben Ripley for future missions and suspect he would be a very good selection for Operation

One last item: I am somewhat concerned about this Mike Brezinski character. How much does he know? Let's discuss options.

Sincerely,

# Acknowledgments

Once again, I am indebted to the incredibly talented Anjan Sarkar for his tireless work on this project. This isn't just a graphic novel, folks. It's a work of art. To that end, I also have to thank the equally incredibly talented Lucy Ruth Cummins and Krista Vitola for shepherding this project, as well as all the other fine folks at Simon & Schuster: Justin Chanda, Erin Toller, Beth Parker, Roberta Stout, Kendra Levin, Alyza Liu, Anne Zafian, Lisa Moraleda, Jenica Nasworthy, Chava Wolin, Chrissy Noh, Ashley Mitchell, Brendon MacDonald, Nadia Almahdi, Christina Pecorale, Victor Iannone, Emily Hutton, Theresa Pang, Dainese Santos, Tom Daly, and Michelle Leo. Plus, my amazing agent, Jennifer Joel.

Thanks are also due to my fellow authors (and support group): Sarah Mlynowski, Rose Brock, James Ponti, Julie Buxbaum, Max Brallier, Gordon Korman, Christina Soontornvat, Karina Yan Glaser, Alyson Gerber, and Julia DeVillers.

This book wouldn't have happened without the exceptional contributions of Emma Chanen.

On the home front, thanks (and much love) to Ronald and Jane Gibbs; Suzanne, Darragh, and Ciara Howard; and finally, Dashiell and Violet, the best kids any parent could ever ask for. I love you all!